MY FIRST LOVER

MY FIRST LOVER

FERDILA OUATTARA-UCHE

Ferdila Ouattara-Uche
My First Lover

Published by Spines Publishing Platform
ISBN: 979-8-89691-090-9

To my First Lover, my Master, My Lord, and Savior Jesus Christ. I cannot imagine what life would have been without Him.

To my destiny helpers, people sent my way by my Master to help me in many ways. My journey was made easier because of their guidance, prayers, support, and more.

FOREWORD

My First Lover is the story of an African mother who decides to share her life story with her daughter. She uses her narrative to encourage and guide her daughter through the pain of a broken relationship. The mother shows her scars and gives invaluable nuggets of wisdom that she hopes her daughter can use in her journey to find love.

She relates the various love languages Gary Chapman defines to God's love languages. The narrative is touching and gripping as the author shares the complexities of relationships and the traps of youthful lusts. It unearths the humanness and touches on our choices and consequences in love and marriage decisions.

In this book, different life lessons are interwoven with major life principles. She draws out the lessons learnt in her journey of marriage life and highlights the journey of a traumatic marriage, divorce, and restoration.

The author's relationship and affection for her First Lover is tangible on the pages. It is a great read for people going through varying forms of marriage crisis and divorce. It is also educative for young ones yet to make critical life decisions as marriage.

The book will leave you reflecting on your life and on that of others in different relationships. It will make you vigilant and thoughtful in your relationship decision process. You will be touched by the love of her first Lover and will reflect on your own relationship with Him.

The book, my First Lover, evokes different emotions in the reader and ultimately serves as a tool to birth healing for those who have been in any way affected in one relationship mishap or the other.

Read it thoughtfully and prayerfully, and share the lessons with as many as possible.

God bless you for sharing these truths with your daughter and many other daughters worldwide.

Pastor Hannah Abrahams-Appiah.
Pastor/ Counsellor/Author.

CONTENTS

Loved by a Consistent Lover

*As life goes by with its share of challenges and
celebrations,
I have come to realize that some things will remain
constant.
The first that comes to my mind, is Your love that is so
consistent.
So steadfast that it decided to overlook my wrong deeds
and actions.
You loved me even when I was dirty, swimming in filth,
Your affection chased, pursued, and pushed me to yield,
Your faithfulness can be seen all over me just like a shield,
You washed me clean and wrapped me with dignity like
gold gilt.
What can I say? I do not even know why I am cherished
by You, my First Lover.
All I know is, You despised Your Throne and came to
give Your life as a sacrifice.
To atone for my sins, and redeem me for the Father by
paying the highest price.
All I can say is, this life You purchased with Your life is
yours forever.*

PROLOGUE

You do not know me, and you probably never heard about me. My name is Kavodiya. I was born somewhere in Africa. I am a mother of three wonderful biological children, and married to an awesome man who threw me a surprise party to celebrate my half-a-century life journey. All my children were there, the biological, but also several others God gave me by divine connection. Women and men who honored me for playing an important role in their lives. People who are calling me mother blood ties notwithstanding. My mother was there, at seventy-four, celebrating me with others.

I consider myself blessed, not only because of my family but because of other achievements, including the support provided to orphans and widows in several countries. The organization I founded is currently running four orphanages with several hundreds of children supported with feeding, and schooling, but most essentially with spiritual and emotional support to be equipped to live a successful life.

A songwriter said: 'I could have missed, I could have fallen by the wayside.' These lines summarize what I have been through, only that in my case, I fell several times. My life journey was quite complex but interesting because of the many lessons I learned over the years. I failed many times. I was so down at some points that I considered quitting, but here am I, alive and even celebrated.

The same song further says, 'You were always there to help me.' Just like that songwriter, someone was there to help me, to pick me up anytime I fell. That someone, is the subject of the following chapters. Just like the title of this book suggests, I call

Him my First Lover, for so many reasons that I will explain later. But I also call him so many other names, because I have to discover so many facets of His personality. He is unsearchable. Trying to know Him is a lifetime endeavor because I do not think any human being can ever be able to fathom Him in His entirety. However, in His infinite magnanimity, He reveals parts of His personality to those who care to seek to know Him better. I have come to understand that there is nothing sweeter than partnering with Him in life, and for the partnership to work, I need to be cognizant of His Person and His ways.

I call Him Abba; it is a Hebrew word that means Father. But the meaning of "Father" in Hebrew is more encompassing than the English rendition. Abba is Father, but He is also a provider and a protector, just like any good father should be. He is indeed my Father, caring for me for so long, providing for me, and protecting me.

I call Him Adonai or Jehovah meaning Lord, Master, or Owner. He is my Master because I surrendered my life to Him some decades ago and I want to follow His command at every point in my life. My life is no longer my own, it is His.

I call Him Asafo Yehowa, the Lord of Host in Twi. I call Him Elombe, my Defender, in Lingala. I call Him Olugbeja, the One who fights for me in Yoruba.

I call Him my First Lover because He was the first to love me. He knew me before I was formed in my mother's womb and kept me there until I saw the light of the day. He is my First Lover because He is the number one on the list of people who love me. He loved me even before I loved Him. He loves me unconditionally, despite everything.

As previously stated, this book is about Him and His love for me. But this book is also a letter to my first daughter Zephaniah, who recently had her heart broken by a man she considered to be her first lover. Her tears made me realize that I did not prepare her enough for a time like this. In this book, I am sharing a few of the lessons I learned through the several heartbreaks I went through during part of the five decades of my life.

Reminiscing past seasons of my life took me through an emotional roller coaster which was somehow therapeutic. I had no idea that some of my wounds were still open until I found myself shedding tears while recalling some events.

Writing this letter was a huge blessing to me, and I hope it will bless you, too.

Part One

ENGAGED TO A FICKLE MAN

Chapter One

HE LOVES ME DESPITE ALL

My daughter, it is hard to believe that you have grown to become the wonderful and strong woman I am watching. Twenty-three years ago, when we met for the first time after a few hours of labor in the hospital, you became one of the closest people to me. I saw every step of your transformation process, and I must confess that I am amazed at what God is doing. You are so beautiful inside out—your dark, shining skin, ridged neck, wonderful smile, and above all, your eyes are beautiful to behold.

I am so saddened that these eyes are filled with tears as we speak. For me, it is even harder to believe today that this man you introduced to me a few months ago and who vowed that he was madly in love with you, cheated on you and broke your heart.

I sometimes ask myself why men do such things. Why would someone hurt someone he professed to love and then come back and claim that it was a mistake? How can someone sleep with another person by mistake? I do not understand how these things happen, but unfortunately, you are not the first lady going through the pain you are going through today, and let me tell you that this will also come to pass. You feel like dying today because your heart is shattered into a hundred pieces. But let me reassure you that this heart will soon love again.

This made me realize that I never explained my relationship experiences to you. You asked me several times why I left your biological father, and I refused to tell you what happened. But I think today is a good day for me to tell you about my mistakes, especially the lessons I learned on this journey of relationships.

My journey, as you already know, was not a smooth one, but my prayer for you is that you will have the smoothest journey ever. I pray that you succeed where I failed and that you will avoid all the mistakes I made. I pray that the God I serve will keep you and your life partner in His mighty hands. I decree that you will not fail in Jesus' name, and your marriage will make heaven proud. It will be an example for many generations to follow. For you, there will be no more breakups and no divorce once you finally settle. The Lord our God will continue to guide and counsel you. When the time comes to get married, you will marry the right man, and when the time comes to have children, the children will come. The Lord will supply all your needs including the spiritual ones, the emotional, material, and physical needs. You will have no reason to regret meeting your spouse-to-be. Anytime you will think about your decision to get married when you finally do, thanksgiving songs will come from your lips.

I pray God will direct you to your partner. He will be a strong support for you. He will help you discover who you are and help you to achieve what God has ordained for your life. You will be his helpmeet, greatest cheerleader, confidant, and mother of his children. He will love and sacrifice for you; you will respect and follow him as he follows the Lord Jesus. You two will overcome challenges, and you will come out victorious and stronger from every battle. Your home will be a house of the Lord, a house of

Prayer where the Word of God will be placed on every lintel and wall to remind your children of the faithfulness of Jehovah. When men around you will say there is a casting down, you will say there is a lifting up. Your posterity will be mighty upon the Earth. These children will beautify you like bridal jewels and remain a reason to celebrate the goodness of the Lord.

Remain ever blessed, you the first fruit of my womb.

My mother, your grandmother, told you several stories about my childhood, how I was smart in school, and how I made my parents proud. I must say that I was lucky to be born into the household of this prayer warrior who initiated me into prayer at a tender age. I remember kneeling next to her not knowing what she was saying and who she was talking to in this position of reverence. Despite my ignorance, this God I did not know came to me in a beautiful dream I will never forget. My mother could not understand the dream, so we went to a man of God who explained the message from God. It was glorious, and I think that is when the enemy started attacking my destiny.

The devil is the enemy of every destiny. If God has a plan for your life, you can be sure that the enemy will try his best to sabotage the realization of this plan. The weapon the devil used to destroy my destiny at that tender age was sexual impurity.

I cannot remember the exact dates, but I think just a few days or weeks after I was told what God was expecting from me, I was for the first time in my life exposed to pornography. My mother told you that I was a late sleeper. I loved television, and even if we only had one channel back then, I would stay until the last program was aired. Then my father bought a video player and a few cassettes that we were watching. When I say we; I need to explain that besides my parents' three children, our house was home to more than twenty people: cousins, nephews, and family friends who needed support to finish secondary school or university in the city where we were staying. A full house that unfortunately, was not dedicated to Jesus Christ. My mother was the only Christian in the house. The only altar to Jehovah was the one she erected in her room, where I occasionally joined her.

An important lesson I want you to take from that experience is the need to have an altar to Jesus Christ to which all the members of the household bow. That is the only way to ensure everyone has the same spirit and values.

My mother never knew that my cousins were watching porn late into the night when the parents were not around. That is how, one night, I stumbled on them when I came out of my room. I was only four years old. They did not chase me out and could not be bothered when I sat to watch the movie with them. Events like that will repeat themselves a few times, and I remember that at least once, my brother, who would have been two or three years old at that time, was also there watching. I did not understand the gravity of what was happening then and the impact of those films on my life until later on, when I started battling with thoughts of sexual impurity.

A few months later, one of the young people staying in our home because of his schooling forced himself onto me. I was not even five years old then. I realize today that the devil was all out to kill something inside of me.

Sexual immorality is a powerful tool that the enemy is using to destroy destinies, and I can tell you that from a fact. Fast forward to a few years later, I was now a teenager. We still had several people in the house, including a cousin a few years older than me. This boy and I caressed on several occasions, unknown to my parents. –

I was a victim of sexual immorality thoughts for decades, even after I surrendered my life to Jesus. I battled to keep myself pure, not knowing that the thoughts I entertained for years were authorizations I was giving to demons to oppress me. To make things worse, I was more and more exposed to movies not tagged as pornographic per se but with nude scenes because the movie industry was growing, and so was entertainment through videos, DVDs, cable, and later the internet.

When I entered my first serious relationship, I was born again, and we started on the purity ground. His name was John. We connected for months without any physical contact, only by chatting when we had the opportunity to meet. Back then, we did not have mobile phones, but we met and discussed on weekends when I was not busy at school, and he was not at work. The connection was real, and I believe God wanted us to get married, but after some time, while waiting to start my first year in University, I became idle. I had so much free time, and he created opportunities for us to meet more often. That is how the devil entered into our relationship. John first asked me for a kiss which I happily gave because I was also attracted to him.

Reflecting on it today, I realize it was so easy for me to fall into sin because I was no longer attending Christian fellowship meetings at school. My prayer life at that point was at its lowest level. That kiss was supposed to remain the only one before we got married, multiplied into several other ones that progressively led us to caress ourselves until we started having sexual intercourse.

Suddenly, the relationship became more tense and more complex. People who were previously in favor of our marriage started opposing it. Things became so tough that we ended up not getting married. I now realize that the main reason this happened was the access we gave to the devil. Our relationship was no longer grounded on Christ our Master, so it became easy for the devil to destroy it.

I would like to give you more details about this relationship because I have learned so much from it. I will spare you the details of how we met and fell in love. You know I am a hopeless romantic; however, romance is not what I want to highlight here, but rather the numerous lessons I learned.

I was far from Him, so many years later, I realized His hand was the only reason I was alive and well. I couldn't sing or do anything during church services, but I spent hours there praying and fellowshipping with the Holy Spirit when the temple was empty. Would it be weird if I told you that I am very fond of those days that were supposed to be the darkest moments of my young life? The Lord's presence and joy I was feeling were like a constant balm on my soul. I enjoyed every bit of it. People around me noticed a 180-degree change in my life, and I remember people, total strangers, followed me to church just because they saw the joy I was exulting.

The main lesson I learned from that season of my life is that, Jesus Christ is and will always be my First Lover. My First Lover because, He was the first to love me even before I was formed in my mother's womb. My First Lover because, the Bible says He loved me first even when I was in sin. My First Lover because, among the people who professed or are professing their love to me, He will always be the number one because He gave His life for me. I do not see who else can die for me but Jesus.

Chapter Two

I LOVE HIM BECAUSE HE LOVED ME FIRST

During that period of my life, I started experiencing great blessings from my Jesus. One thing about Him is that He is a giver who gives His life for you. So, any other needs you have will always be covered.

When all these events happened, I told you I was waiting for the University to open for freshers. When I finally resumed school, I was addicted to His presence. I remember reaching the University at five a.m. to ensure I could reserve a seat in the amphitheater for my friends and myself. Once this was done, I would look for an empty room to spend quality time with my Jesus before the teacher's arrival—sweet moments of fellowship with Jesus, my dear daughter.

A key lesson for you here is that one of Jesus's love languages is quality time. The Father, the Son, and the Holy Spirit love to spend time with us—quality time, quiet time during which they will speak to you, teach you how to go, and comfort you when you are down.

I spent hours in these classrooms between 5 and 7:30 am enjoying their presence. This is the opportunity for me to tell you to consistently and intentionally create time to have fellow-ship with Jesus who is my First Lover, no matter what. The world is so time-consuming nowadays. It's the era of social media, the era of any solicitation on your time disputing your availability for the Master. Besides, the older you grow, the heavier the responsibilities on your shoulders. You will soon get married, and then your life will change. Your husband will expect you to care for him and give him part of your time. Later, the children will come and demand your time. Not to mention when you get a job and have to spend the rest of your day somewhere just because you need to make a living. When all this happens, the temptation will be for you to tell the Master that you do not have enough time for Him, and because He is so gentle, He will never insist. He will just let you be. He will not complain like your husband if he is neglected, He will not cry like the children, He will not shout like your boss, He will just be silent and observe you from afar. This could lead you to forget Him and finally decide that two hours per week of your time is more than enough for Him.

I am warning you, never make that mistake. Please be inten-tional about the time you allocate to Him. The reason is that, He alone can help you navigate all the seasons of your life. He alone can help you satisfy the other people asking for your time and attention. Without Him, you will fail as a wife, as a mother, and as a worker. No books you will read on marriage, parenting, and your career can give you the kind of advice He provides. I am not saying that books are wrong, and you know I am a massive aficionado of books, I am just saying that often, without His help, you will even have challenges to grasp the truths that the books are exposing. Please keep Him in your life; keep Him closer and closer by the day. Make time for Him.

Returning to my story, I told you that most of my prayer points were about my local church. He also asked me to pray for the friends around me. Acts of service is another language of my

Master Jesus. The establishment of His Kingdom on Earth is His primary concern. If you love Him, His concern should become your concern. If you love Him, you will be part of the people serving Him. You know how I have been serving Him all these years, doing anything I could for His Church. I am doing that first because I love Him, but also because I know that's one of the ways He wants me to express my love to Him.

Many people profess their love for Him, but when you check their actions or motivations, it's hard to say if they love Him.

People who genuinely love Him, love His Kingdom. They want to see it come on Earth as it is in Heaven, and they try their best to advance it by preaching His love to others. People who love Him, love His house. They want to be there as often as possible, and they want to see it decorated, befitting for the King that He is. People who love Him, love His children and support them. People who love Him, keep His commandments and do His bidding.

You cannot say you love Him when the only things that matter to you are the things you can get from Him. Imagine yourself in a relationship with someone who only comes to you when he needs something. He only does things for you because he expects something in return. Many Christians are just like that in the house of God. Their only motivation to be there is the miracle they are expecting from God. They are only serving God because of the reward attached to the service. Their love is purely transactional, and the day God does not meet their expectations is when they decide not to love Him again.

The truth is God is a Rewarder, but He only rewards acceptable service. And when you analyze the requirements of an acceptable service, you will realize that the only acceptable service is the one provided out of love. To be acceptable, a service must be done willingly, joyfully, consistently, and tirelessly. The only way to meet these criteria is to be love-driven, and that's what our

Father expects from us. Only love can make someone render a joyful service consistently without murmuring or feeling tired or frustrated. He will undoubtedly reward, but reward should not be our first goal, but Himself. By the way, He is far greater than any reward; He told Abraham He was His Exceedingly Great Reward. If the Master Himself is your reward, you have everything.

Another love language of the Master is words of appreciation, the fruits of our lips declaring His attributes, His goodness, and His faithfulness. We read in the Bible that King David mastered this art and suddenly became God's darling. Take time to tell Him who He is to you and to express your heartfelt gratitude for what He does for you. I know it is sometimes difficult, but over the years, I have learned a few tips that I would like to share with you. First, ensure your heart is full of gratitude before expressing anything to Him. The fruits of your lips must be an expression from your heart. When what you are saying and what you have in your heart are not connected, it irritates Him. A tip I have been using to fill my heart with gratitude is to ponder on his acts of kindness towards me. I often write lists of things to remember them. These gratitude lists are powerful tools to trigger sincere thanksgiving. The truth is that, our human nature tends to live in the moment and focus on current happenings. Your circumstances will often tell you there is no reason to praise or worship Him, but in moments like that, take the time to start a gratitude list or review an old one, and you will automatically switch to worship mode. The truth is, our Lover is so Good and so Faithful.

I recently heard a man of God preaching on a revelation he got, and it tremendously blessed me. He said that God's goodness is why He designs excellent plans for us. His goodness is like an architect drawing plans for a house. Then, His faithfulness takes over to build the house. His faithfulness is why He never gives up on the plans and ensures the house is constructed even when we are not consistent in keeping our part of the deal. Like my Father in the Lord always says, "You will thank God well if you think well." You will find thousands of reasons to be grateful, starting with the fact that you are not in the grave right now. How many people are dying daily who are far better than you would ever be?

I know that Jesus is the only reason I am alive and well. If He only left me without protection for a second, I would have been long gone, because my enemies have been trying so hard even before I was born to get rid of me.

I will bless the Lord at all times, and His praise shall continually be in my mouth.

Another important tip is to ensure you speak about His goodness and say the words. Do not just meditate about it in your heart. He can indeed hear your heart, but the question is, what is stopping you from using your mouth to state it? There is nothing more frustrating than a lover who decides to keep his feelings in his heart without expressing them because he assumes that the subject of his love already knows about his feelings. Worship is about expressing what you feel for your God. It's about offering sacrifices to your God; one of the sacrifices is continuous worship with the fruits of your lips giving thanks to His name. By the way, the Master expresses His love to us daily. Anytime you read the Bible, God will tell you how much He loves you. If you can hear Him, you will hear His voice saying how much He loves you.

Another way to express your love to our Master is by giving. The Bible says because He loved us, He gave His son. That is how He operates, and that is how He expects us to operate. Your love for Him must push you to give Him your best. He expects nothing less than your best because when He gives, He gives His best. Jesus was His best; He did not hesitate to give Him away for us. He will always ask for your best.

In the Bible, we read about how Cain failed to give Him his best, while Abel did. When God wanted Abraham to give Him something special, He asked him for Isaac, who was his best. The good news is, just as Abraham came down from the mountain with both Isaac and a sworn blessing, in the same way, all your sincere giving's' will trigger God to give you more than you gave. He is expecting you to devote the best of your resources to Him. After all, He gave them to you. He expects the best of your time, the best of your money, the best of your talent, in short, the best of your life. Giving your money while you keep your talents for purposes other than Him does not amount to anything in His sight. He is unequivocal about what He wants; He wants your heart first, and any other giving must derive from that heart that is devoted to Him. When He has your heart, you will not struggle to give Him anything.

You will not give grudgingly. He hates anything given to Him while grudging. He wants you to give bountifully and joyfully. I recently listened to a man of God who made me laugh hard. He was jokingly telling the congregation that Christians frown anytime it is time to give in church. The offering time is a time of sorrow for many because their hearts are bleeding as they are relinquishing whatever they brought as a sacrifice. Giving without rejoicing is a waste. In my opinion, it is better not to give. My advice to you, my daughter, is to ensure joy is in your heart anytime you are giving anything to the Master; be it your time, your talent, or your resources. Anything you give without your joy being in place, is not accepted by Him.

Like I told you, when you give Him, He gives back to you. During that dark season of my life, I gave Him my heart, my time, my worship, and He just blew my mind.

My mother's dream for me was to travel out of the country for my studies. It was the dream of several of my friends from secondary school, and my first year at the university to travel outside the country for further studies. I must confess that it was somehow my dream also, but because of my reality, I never allowed that dream to germinate in my mind. I never asked for it or prayed for it because it was impossible considering the circumstances. My father was late, my mother was raising her three children with what she was making from her fish-selling business. Although she ensured we did not lack anything, we were not rich, and I knew we could never afford the fees to study out of the country. Several students with well-to-do families were trying to get out of the country too. The lines in front of the French Embassy were popular because people would start queuing there from as early as 4a.m to enable them to access the embassy when it opened at 8am.

I remember reading an article from a newspaper about how a young girl was killed by bandits who robbed her because she had woken up early morning and was walking to the embassy alone in the streets at an ungodly hour, because of her appointment at the embassy. I was, therefore, keeping my expectations low, being content with the fact that I got admitted to the Law faculty. After all, I could have been denied a visa just like many of my friends. My mother, on the other end, kept hoping and praying that I would travel. She asked my late father's friends who could help if they could find a scholarship for me, but nobody would or could help. She contacted an international insurance company where she was keeping her savings and asked if they could help. I remember us visiting the white lady managing my mother's account and my mother telling her that she needed help for me to get admission to a University in France. I will never forget the answer she gave to my mother:

It is too late for an admission. French Universities start
their admission and registration processes in January.
This is September. Even my son, who is a French citizen,
struggled to be accepted. There is no way your daughter

can get admitted to a French University for the academic year starting in October. It is just impossible.

When we left the lady's office, I told myself that at least this would help my mother realize that there was no hope. I was worried because she was restless about this issue of travel. I now realize that God was pushing her because, against all odds, she continued to seek help, being fully persuaded that my destiny was to travel out of my country. I need to clarify here that my mother was not the kind of person obsessed with leaving Africa, far from that. Before then, she had visited Europe several times for business trips when my father was alive. My mother was a serial entrepreneur with several business streams before my father became sick. His sickness lasted for an extended period, and my mother had to pay for dialysis sessions twice a week to keep him alive. I remember that each session was worth hundreds of thousands of CFA. By the time my father died, my mother's business resources had been depleted. So, no, it was not about me leaving the country. It was more about giving me all the chances to succeed academically.

The public University system of my country was a mess because of the regular strikes organized by violent members of student unions. I remember how one of them threatened me when I protested how they interrupted our teacher one day. These students threatened everybody: the teachers, the university staff members, and the students. In the name of fighting for our rights, they had become the worst nightmare of the university system, manipulated by the politicians who were sending them. For years, the students' learning times were stalled, they were not able to have enough teaching time before they had to sit for examinations. By the time I started my first year in the Law faculty, I was with friends who had been waiting to sit for an examination to begin their second year to no avail. My mother did not want that for me, and she was trying her best to find a way out of this mess.

One Wednesday morning, I was home because the student union had ordered a strike action. Our landline rang. It was my mother. She asked me to meet with her in someone else's office. She gave me the address and told me to hurry up. I did and met with her in front of a particular building. We entered and waited for some time, then we were introduced to the office of a lady who seemed to be the overall boss. The lady was a supplier of my mother. She explained how my mother had told her about me and how brilliant I was. She promised to help me and started making calls. Before I realized what was happening to me, I was on the plane exactly a week later, on my way to the southern part of France.

Exactly one week was all it took for my First Lover to open that academic door many people had hoped for for years. The process started with that phone call on a Wednesday morning, and the following Wednesday at 10 p.m., I was on a flight to France. The Lord granted me favor in the sight of this lady I was meeting for the first time that faithful Wednesday morning. She used her influence, wealth, and connection to get me the necessary travel documents and registration with a renowned law faculty. She paid for my ticket and even gave me some money for my feeding.

The Psalmist said, "When the Lord turned again the captivity of Zion, we were like them in that dream...." It was indeed like a dream. It took just one week, exactly seven days, for me to enter into a blessing that many people had been praying for, for years to obtain.

Over the years, I have understood that when my First Lover wants to bless, He specializes in sudden blessings. These are what men will call 'miracles' because it is evident that only the Hand of Jehovah God can perform it.

Two days before my travel, John came to visit me. He did not ask for forgiveness; he even blamed me for not telling him I had plans to travel. He introduced himself back into my life, and I accepted him without a second thought. After all, I was convinced he was my husband. We agreed on our next course of action. I was going to travel to France for my studies, and he would join me later and continue his studies.

When I sat on that plane heading towards Marseille, my joy was complete; I was over the moon. My human lover was back, and my academic destiny had opened up to great promises. What else could a 19-year-old girl ask for?

Chapter Three

HE GUIDES ME THROUGH THE GREEN PASTURES

Upon arrival in France, my two lovers were in my life. My First Lover, Jesus Christ was with me, while I regularly contacted John via letters and phone calls.

My Lord Jesus ensured I stayed glued to Him. He directed my steps to the correct set of people, young Christians on fire for Jesus, and I must say that the time I spent in that country helped me to get closer to the Master Jesus. Unlike in my own country, Christianity was a choice and not a trend people were following. The norm in my country was to have almost everybody going to church on Sunday. In France, I could not help but notice how quiet the streets were when I was trekking to church. People were sleeping, enjoying their sleep-in time. The few people on the roads were cyclists passionate about their bicycles who did not care about my Jesus. I was not shocked because I knew Europe had driven very far away from God, but I was sad to see that a continent once passionate for Jesus had become so cold and agnostic a few generations down the line.

But because of this general atmosphere of coldness for the things of God, most of the people who were following Jesus were doing it by choice, not out of necessity, but from a sincere heart of devotion. I will never forget some of our youth meetings where the presence of the Lord was so sensible, tangible, and palpable, just because it was a gathering of people thirsty for Him. I remember three of our friends who were evicted from the hostel room where they were praying and decided to pray in their car during the winter. A genuine craving and passion for Jesus that I hardly saw in my country. These were beautiful times, and I will forever be grateful to Jesus for leading me to these people and maintaining my love for Him, even when I was far from home. I am even more thankful today that I have visited several countries in the world where I have seen Africans disconnected from Jesus in the name of "no time." People who used to serve Him back in their countries of origin, people who prayed for God to help them get visas, and who decided, once they had landed in Western countries, that Jesus was not worth following. The truth is they were following Jesus for something, and now that He had given it to them, they couldn't see the need to continue being with Him.

Unfortunately, our churches in Africa are full of people like that, who want to see the Hand of God without seeking His face or His heart—consumer Christians who only want to receive from God and never give. "Give me bread and butter," Christians who see God as a milky cow.

The way God directed my steps to the right people was miraculous. I landed in Marseille and stayed there for a few weeks, It took time for me to get a room in a hostel in Aix-en-Provence, the city where my university was. I therefore had to travel back and forth from where I was to where my university was, and I remembered seeing twice or thrice a young black lady looking so chic. She was walking on the streets of Aix-en, and I couldn't help but notice her. I remember my "cousin," the nephew of my destiny helper, who registered me with the university, telling me one day when we were sitting on the bus, to look for this girl. Her hairstyle showed that she was very much connected to

Africa. My cousin said, "She will show you the right spots in the city." He was joking, but he did not know that she was meant to become one of my best friends.

When I finally got a room at the hostel, I moved from Marseille to Aix-en, and after dropping off my luggage, I took the bus to the market to buy pots and sweaters because the cold was settling in. Because it was a market, I knew I needed to bargain, but I had no idea about the average prices. So I told myself I needed someone to help, and as soon as this thought came to my mind, the lady I saw several times from the bus appeared in front of me. I asked her if she could help me with the pricing of the goods I needed. She said yes and helped me while I was buying what I needed. When we were done, she told me her hostel was close to the market and invited me for lunch. I followed her to her room, and while there, I saw books on her shelf, including some by Charles Spurgeon! This triggered my curiosity. She was reading Spurgeon's books. Who was this girl? A few seconds later, I saw a Bible verse in a frame: "Guard your heart with all diligence, for from it flow springs of life" (Psalm 4:23). This scripture was one of those my Lord gave me when I was going through hell after the rejection by John. I couldn't resist it anymore and asked her:

Are you a Christian?

"Yes," she replied. I thought there was no chance I could meet a serious Christian so randomly.

"Where do you pray, I asked her?"

She replied, "I am from the Assemblies of God."

I shouted out of surprise.

This could only be God. To meet a sister in the Lord randomly in the market. The fact that I noticed her without knowing who she was weeks before, was already a mystery. In a city of hundreds of thousands of people, my eyes went to this lady several times. I finally met her and realized that she was a sister. Our encounter was divinely ordained. My Lover Jesus was telling me that He was ordering my steps.

My new lady friend, Tabitha, was the one who introduced me to the student fellowship and the church I attended all my years in Aix-en-Provence. The Bible says, "I will instruct you and teach you how you shall go; I will guide you with my eyes upon you" (Psalm 32: 8). This scripture was once again fulfilled in my life.

I met wonderful people in the student union who challenged my love for Jesus and made it look like I was joking, people who could do anything for the Lord. I was tremendously blessed. Meanwhile, I started planning to have John join me in pursuing his studies in France.

I forgot to mention that John was a brilliant man with an Associate Degree in Economics. His dream was to at least obtain a Master's degree . When we started our courtship, he told me he had to stop because he needed to focus on their family business. He was one of the top scorers of his region for the "A" level examinations, but here he was now with not even with a bachelor degree. I remember telling him to ensure that he could go back to school and earn a degree for himself. I also told him that the family business was a family business and that if I were him, I would not see any future for myself there. By the time he broke up with me, he was attending night classes to obtain a bachelor's degree in business administration. When we reconciled a day before my trip, we agreed that he would join me in France to complete his studies. I started sending him information about the courses, the prices for the schooling, etc. After a few weeks, he became silent. There was no news from him. I was so worried that I told a few friends to help me pray. I could sense that we were drifting apart again.

However, one faithful day in May, he called me and gave me the news that made me overjoyed. He told me:

"We just had a family meeting. We have all agreed that when you come for the summer break, my family will meet your family to pay the dowry."

That day became one of the happiest days of my life. I was over the moon, but about three weeks later, in the beginning of June, I received a letter that shattered my heart. A good friend told me how sorry he was that my relationship with John did not work out. I was reading the letter but couldn't understand what my friend was talking about. He mentioned a marriage between John and my friend, the lady I heard he started dating just a few weeks after breaking up with me. I couldn't believe the news, so I called my mother. She confirmed it and told me how sorry she was. They did not want to let me know of it because she, of all people, knew such news would break me. I couldn't believe my mother. I couldn't believe that the man who called me less than three weeks before could betray me again. The funny thing was, my mother informed me that he was getting married that very day. I called John myself because I needed to hear from him to be sure that these were rumors and nothing else.

When he answered my phone call, his tone and everything were expressing the disdain he had for me. He told me the unthinkable when I asked him why he did not inform me about his marriage plan: He said,

"I was hoping that your family would have told you. I did not think I was the one to tell you."

What? Unbelievable! Betrayed twice by the same man. For the first time in my life, thoughts of suicide crossed my mind. My hostel room was on the fourth floor, and I was asking myself, why not jump? Why not put an end to this pain that is ravaging your heart?

But the God I serve and my First Lover, once again came to my rescue. Tabitha, my friend, the lady I met who took me to the market, came to visit me and decided to stay with me over the weekend. She was there when I cried all the tears I could release out of my body. Two days later, on Monday, I was sitting for my final exams for my first year at the law faculty. How I passed those exams was once again the demonstration of My Father (Abba)'s love for me. I did not fail my exams, I did not die, I survived betrayal and disdain and passed on to the next level of my life. I was hurting and the scar was there, but I was stronger or I believed so.

Another lesson I want to highlight for you my dear daughter is the fact that, this pain that you are feeling today because this man shattered your heart will soon pass. It will not kill you; it will make you stronger. It is part of your building process. Never allow pain to cripple you because your destiny is far beyond what you are currently going through presently. Imagine me giving up on my dreams to become a lawyer that weekend because my heart was in pieces. I would have regretted that decision my entire life. Never allow circumstances to divert you from your destiny. Stay focused despite all things because the event will come to pass, the heartbreak will come to pass, the betrayal will come to pass, the disdain and the humiliation will all come to pass. Never allow your stay in the "pit" to erase your dreams of greatness. It's just one step in the journey of your life, it is not your final destination. From the Bible, we learn that Joseph was thrown into the pit, then he was a slave in Potiphar's house, and from there, he was thrown into prison. But one day, the greatness God showed him when he was seventeen years old, finally manifested. His journey took thirteen years of low and down times which could have succeeded in killing his dreams, but he did not allow it to. He kept his trust in the God who gave him the dreams, and it eventually became his reality.

In June, I had to travel back to my home town, and because John and I were gravitating around the same circles, we met at a wedding. He was with his wife who was obviously pregnant. Remembering this moment now, I realize that they might have felt uncomfortable. The great news is, I did not feel bad. I was happy as usual, anytime I was attending a wedding.

There is something about me and weddings that I cannot explain. The only wedding I attended and I was sad, was during my relationship with John. This happened before I travelled to school in France. It was on February 14th, and I expected to see him there. Unfortunately for me, I waited for him but he did not come. His family members were there at the wedding, my mother was there, almost all the people we knew, except the one I wanted to see. I digressed to narrate this story because it remains what I consider to be the apex of our relationship. So, on February 14th , my lover was not where I was expected to meet him.

To give you a bit of background; because we were not married, we were not supposed to be left alone for a romantic dinner or any outing. This happened before sin came and defiled our union. I left the venue of the wedding sad. One of his best friends told me he was quite busy with the family business because Valentine's Day was a big day and there would be many people and lots of sales, so that, he couldn't make it to the wedding. This was before the era of mobile cell phones so that, he couldn't call and explain why he was absent. When I reached the house with my mother, my brother gave me a package. John had been there. He came directly to my house after closing the business, thinking I would have returned from the wedding. Unknown to him, the couple came late, typical of weddings in Africa, and the guests had to wait hours before they could proceed with the event, but let me leave this comment for another day.

So back to me, receiving my Valentine's package in the house. Inside the package was a teddy bear, a box of chocolate, flowers, and the most poetic note I had ever read. In a nutshell, he was telling me how he was craving to see me. This was pure love, and I couldn't help but cry.

I entered my room with the gifts and felt so sad because it was apparent that we wouldn't see each other that day or so, I thought. It was not about Valentine's Day. It was more about how this felt like a missed opportunity for us to see each other. Back then, I was in boarding school, and the opportunities to meet John were scarce. Missing this chance to see him because he could not make it to the wedding, and I coming too late to my house to meet him felt like a dagger had been put in my heart. I took a shower crying and was lying on my bed when my brother came to tell me that I had a visitor. It was after 10pm.

When I entered our living room, John was sitting there. I will probably never forget the feelings I had at that very moment. The joy and the happiness were out of the world. We couldn't hug or kiss, but our smiles said everything we felt. This man was living about 30km away from my mother's house. He was tired after a long day at work yet, he came to my house to see me and had to leave. On his way to his house on the highway, he decided to return. Why? Because he felt I would be sad and decided that he wanted to make me happy by all means. He told me how as he drove in the opposite direction on the highway, he decided to make a U-turn just to see me. This day will forever stick in my mind because of my intense feelings and emotions and John's sacrifices to see me.

This same John, two years later, at another wedding, was with a wife who was not me, and she was obviously pregnant. Remember, I told you that his wife was a good friend of mine. I exchanged jokes and pleasantries with her. Apparently, he was uncomfortable seeing me, but I was fine. As usual, the Holy

Spirit had done wonders in healing my wounds and I was happy to attend another wedding. Out of genuine concern, I asked him about his examination. I remembered that he was to sit for it that year. He told me he failed and blamed it on the preparations for the wedding. That was the last time I set my eyes on a man who I thought loved me with every fiber of his being, a man whom I was ready to die for, a man who betrayed me twice without giving it a second thought.

Chapter Four

HE MIGHT BE SILENT WHEN I DO NOT ASK HIS VIEWS, BUT HE STILL LOVES ME

During that particular summer holiday, I had a number of suitors coming my way. I was there for two months, and I remember that four men expressed interest in getting married to me. Was it because it was my season for marriage or because some of them were considering prospects of settling in France? I cannot tell, but in any case, my summertime was quite busy.

The first suitor was an excellent friend of mine. He was a student and was someone I had known for years. We were in the same church, and he had never told me previously about his interest in me. That year, he started coming to my mother's house more often than usual, and finally talked to me about his feelings for me. Was he interested in me earlier and did not say anything because he knew I was in a relationship? We were almost the same age, meaning he was relatively young, I think he was 22 when he told me about his feelings for me.

The second suitor was another friend who was a teacher. He was in the same denomination as I was, but he was fellowshipping in another branch. He was ready to settle and get married because he was in his thirties. He told me he had been observing me from afar, and before he could make a move to declare his interest , he heard I was in a relationship with John. He opened up to me during a pilgrimage I made to what is considered to be the birthplace of our church, he told me about his feelings during the long journey.

My third suitor was a Pastor I met during a service in a church where I was invited to sing. The Head Pastor who knew me asked me to minister during a short worship session he was organizing at a prayer night. A few days later, I got a call from the Pastor indicating that someone who attended the vigil wanted to meet me. Because I respected the man of God, I met with this total stranger who started interrogating me about my life and my studies. He insisted he wanted to come and see me in my mother's house. The next thing I knew was, he arrived in our house with a bag of yams and plantains arriving as gifts for my family. We discovered that we were from the same region and spoke the same dialect.

My fourth suitor was also a "businessman" selling school material. My aunty gave me his number and insisted that I should call him but I did not do it. A few days later, I met my aunty again at a wedding. She insisted that I call him and was shouting at me, insinuating that I may miss a good opportunity if I did not call him. I ended up calling him just to have my peace of mind. He came to my mother's house to visit me one day. He was in his late twenties and was ready to settle down in marriage.

A season will always come in a woman's life when men will approach you for various reasons. Some want you in their life just to have fun, some want to get married.

The first lesson I want to draw from my relationship experiences is that, none of these suitors came to me just to have fun because they knew I was not the type of young lady you can just play around with.

All the relationships I ever had, had marriage in view, and even though not all of them led to marriage, the objective was always well-defined from the onset. People will treat you the way you want them to treat you. I know the trend nowadays is to sleep around with you before even thinking about marriage, but I want to insist on the fact that any child of God, and daughter of Zion, should focus on the fact that marriage is the goal, and God desires that we keep the marriage bed undefiled. Being a girlfriend or a 'friend with benefits' should never be the goal of your relationship. If marriage is the goal, you will only attract men who want to marry you. Yet, if you are open to other options other than marriage, men with different motivations than marriage will show up.

Let me use this opportunity to say that married men must be a 'no-go' area when it comes to dating and marriage for any Christian lady. Any Christian girl dating a married man is bringing curses upon herself.

Reason being that, firstly, you are making a bold statement into the spirit realm and even to the world around you that, you have no consideration for the Institution called Marriage. Something you despise cannot come your way. Sometimes, these young ladies are praying for the wife of their boyfriend to die, which is pure wickedness and should not even cross the mind of someone who calls herself a Christian. The excuse of "he said he will get divorced soon" which some give is not justifiable and cannot bail them out. The man is married before God and before men. If he is planning to divorce, let him divorce first before anything can start between you and him.

May God help you not to be the reason why a man is getting a divorce. The Bible clearly states that, what you sow is what you will reap (paraphrased). If you sow the seed of separation in a marriage, be ready to reap separation at some point when you are the one who is married.

The second reason why I am saying that you are calling curses upon your life is the fact that, the wife of this man may be cursing you every day for ruining her marriage. Believe me when I tell you that these curses are not causeless. She definitely has a case. You may be the main reason why her home is troubled, or you are at least contributing to the trouble in the marriage. I am not saying that the married man does not have his share of charges against him; I am just speaking to you, my daughter, to draw your attention to the role you are playing in this scenario. The tears of the married woman will be like a curse upon your head, and if the children are affected, their tears will also speak against you in the realm of the spirit, which is even more dangerous.

I do not know how the church of nowadays is harboring a generation of selfish people who do not care about anything but themselves. Church members and even Pastors can kill others for their comfort and disregard the interests of others. Christ, our Master, my First Lover, was never selfish and will never be, and we are to emulate him. There seems to be new wave of Christian ladies praying for their married boyfriends to divorce their wives. There seems to be also a new generation of Pastors who are supporting such people with their prayers. These things do not have their place in the Body of Christ. God will never be happy with such requests and attitudes.

Back to the lessons I learned during that season of my life. **Lesson number two**: Marriage is not child's play. Take time to ask God. Choosing whom you will marry is a decision that will affect your entire life; it should not be trivialized.

I am saying this because one of my biggest mistakes this season was not being focused. I cannot explain what happened, but I was not spiritually focused. I think the fact that I was on leave and the exhilaration of being the center of attraction for so many men got me carried away. I do not remember taking time out to pray seriously about marriage. I only remember attending wedding after wedding and getting increasingly excited about the idea of finally settling down. I was more interested in making my own analysis of the right person I believed was for me. My stay was relatively short, but before I boarded the plane to return to my studies in France, my mind was already made up on whom I would marry in just two months.

My friend of the same age was off the table because he was too young and unprepared to settle down. Committing to a relationship with him would have meant waiting for at least five or six years before marriage. It involved the time he took to get a university degree and find a job. Besides, I never had any romantic interest in him, so I politely declined his request and asked him to remain my friend.

The teacher was one of the options I seriously considered. I must confess that among all the suitors I met that summer, he was the most mature. I enjoyed his company because he was a sound Christian who knew what he wanted in life. Unfortunately for him, I was not physically attracted to him. He was very tall, and the short lady that I was, did not see herself standing beside this tall man for life.

Regarding suitor number three, who was the Pastor from my region. He was in the right age range, was in his late twenties. He was also the most well-to-do among all of them. His visits to my house were never without gifts and the fact that he was from my region, was an asset for people like my grandmother who was staying with us for a few weeks. He was number one on her list, but something disqualified him for me. One day, as we were speaking, he asked me how long I was intending to study. I told him that I was going back for my second year and that after that, I would have two additional years for a law degree, and that I wanted to go for a fifth year to specialize. He clearly expressed his disapproval of these long years of studies. He wanted to marry as soon as possible and asked me to consider other options for my studies. The day we had that conversation was the day I discarded him from the list of potential husbands for me. I did not tell him right away. Months later, when I was back in France, he sent me a letter explaining how he couldn't wait for me to be back and for us to get married and preach the gospel of Jesus together. I replied with a polite letter explaining that I was honored by the fact that he considered me a potential wife, but I did not think I would be up to the task because I had so many years of studies left.

I settled for the suitor number four, the businessman. He was broke, he had no money and never gave me a gift. He was a school dropout selling school materials on a small table in a market. I do not remember seriously praying about the decision to settle with him , but my mind was at peace about getting married to him, at least that is what I thought back then. Come to think of it, I realize that what attracted me to him was probably his **vulnerability.** Christian should be spiritual enough for his or her soul to be subdued to the spirit man within them. Unfortunately, many Christians nowadays are controlled by their emotions, their intellect, and by the desires of their bodies and not by their spirts which is connected to God. Emotional connection is easy when two people are spiritual. They are led by the same principles and live in the same realm.

The third element is, of course, the physical attraction. I am not talking about so-called compatibility here but about attraction. It is safe to say that what attracts me, might not attract you and vice versa. Beauty, they say is in the eyes of the beholder. I have an issue with a generation that wants to establish a universal standard of beauty. For me, beauty could be short, big nose, dark skin, a nice smile, and gentleness. Beauty can also mean a tall man with a straight nose, light skin, and a straight face for someone else. What moves me in a man might repulse you, so I warn you. Do not ever allow people to decide for you on who you are settling with. Friends may advise you to consider a man because they find him cute or tell you not to consider someone just because "he does not look good." You might land in the wrong relationship or miss out on the love of your life if you do not listen to your reactions and feelings around the person. Physical attraction is important, but it should not be the first criterion to consider and should never be the only one. The fact is, physical attraction comes and goes. It fluctuates with time. You can meet a man to whom you are not attracted today, but a few weeks later, because you have discovered who he is, you will find yourself attracted to him. Never reject a man just because you are not physically attracted at first. Please take the time to get to know him and pray.

Let me take some time to address the issue of money here. Would you consider someone who is poor? A man who cannot make ends meet? On this point, I would like to say that for me, there is poor and there is poor. The first category of poor is a man who lacks and lives in dire conditions because of the bankruptcy of his knowledge of God and God's will for his live. Such a man might remain poor forever, except he realizes where his problem lies, and then engages in the transformation process that will turn him into the one he is supposed to be. If you meet a poor man who does not understand at which stage of his life he is, who does not have a clear understanding of who God says He is, and who cannot tell where he is going by the leading of the Master Jesus, please run away from such a one. And please be careful here, I am not talking about men who are just dreaming out of covetousness, about becoming great, and who never received from God the blueprint or the pathway for their life. Those are very dangerous; they will wreck your destiny if you engage with them. The church is full of such men, who dream of greatness because they heard that God's will for His children is greatness. They have never contended for the understanding of what greatness means in the Kingdom and will probably never comprehend what is required for someone to become great as per the Master's definition.

The second category of poor is those just passing through God's pruning process. I call them the Kings in the making. One of my favorite stories in the Bible is the story of Abigail. Some women in the Bible were very deep in the things of the Spirit and their discernment was amazing. Hannah, Samuel's mother was one of them, another one was Ruth the Moabite, but I want to talk about Abigail. So imagine, you are married to a bully, having to deal with his nonsense every day, but instead of becoming angry and bitter, you turn to become someone the Bible describes as intelligent and beautiful. I know what it is to live with an insensitive man and I know it can kill and destroy every beauty and every brilliance because of the anger and the bitterness triggered by the actions of the man, but here we are with a lady who did not allow the nature of her husband to change her, but rather contended to remain who she was before she got married to a Monster. So, imagine you are married to a bully, hearing about the story of a young man who will probably become King of Israel, but who is now a fugitive, the most wanted man of the Kingdom, a man that the King has vowed to kill. What would you think about this man? I can imagine you saying, it is none of my business, after all, this is politics and it's a men's world. You can even despise him just like Nabal did, and convince yourself that David is probably some adventurer who does not deserve any attention. But here we are with this lady, who was discerning enough to see the king in the making behind the fugitive.

Some men are kings in the making behind one stage of the process they are today. You have kings in the making who are broke, kings in the making who are homeless, kings in the making who are persecuted. David was broke (he was begging Nabal for food); he was homeless, running from one place to another, and he was persecuted. But this lady saw a King, and the Bible says that when she saw David for the first time, she bowed down with her face to the ground. I pray for you my daughter, may God engrace you with the required level of spiritual depth that will help you to discern the king in the making that was sent your way. Your eyes will be opened to see the reality beyond the current circumstances in Jesus' name. 'Kings in the making' usually know who they are because they had an encounter with the prophetic and were communicated the blueprint of their lives. They usually have a deep relationship with the Master because they want to stay on the right track until they can ascend the throne that was revealed to them.

So, please do not be in a haste to discard the broke guy in the church who came to ask if you would consider marrying him. Go to your Father and ask Him who this guy truly is. Does he belong to category one poor like I described earlier who will remain at the same level until Jesus comes back, or is a 'king in the making?' To close this chapter, never allow material things to be your motivation for any decision you are making, including the choice of a husband.

Coming back to my fourth suitor, I ended up marrying him and I must confess that decision I made, almost wrecked my destiny. My lack of seriousness with God during that critical decision-making season of my life came at a very high cost.

Chapter Five

EVEN IN THE PIT, HE STAYS WITH ME

So as already explained, I met my fourth suitor named Olivier because my Aunty insisted that I call him. Note that is not his real name. We started talking and unlike the other suitors, he never portrayed himself as a savior or an opportunity for me. He rather explained all the challenges he was facing. At that period of my life, I did not even know that I had a calling into the helps ministry, but the truth is that since my childhood, the plight of people has always pushed me to try to do something. I remember that one day during my first year in secondary school, there was an incident that happened that makes me realise now that it was pointing to my helps ministry.

During the first weeks of school, the teachers would ask us to pay for the school materials we needed. I have always liked shopping for notebooks, text books, and pens and all I needed for school, and thank God, my parents had enough to afford it.

So back to the incident, we were there in the classroom and the teacher was asking each of us to show her what she asked us to get the week before. She had requested we get a few notebooks, if my memory serves me well. I was pretty excited because I had everything; I showed it to the teacher, who moved to other students. A few minutes after passing my desk, I heard her screaming at another student who did not have the notebooks. When the teacher started shouting, the girl couldn't help crying. She then explained to the teacher that her parents couldn't afford it.

Our school was a public school, but funnily enough, most pupils were from the middle class society, so having someone in school whose parents couldn't afford notebooks was quite strange. The tears of this girl personally broke me. We were about forty or fifty students in the classroom, and even though I had seen her, I had never spoken to her. She was not within my circle of friends. I remember crying silently at my desk after the incident that day and kept telling myself I would ask my father to help her. I did it later when he returned from his office. My dad had a kind heart, and I somehow got what I requested from him. He bought the notebooks for that course and the entire program, and I felt very proud of myself when I walked up to the girl two days later to give her a bag full of notebooks.

I am narrating this story to tell you more about who I am. I was ten years old when this happened, and years later, I understand that the capacity to empathize with people and the giving grace upon my life are great gifts I received from the Master for my assignment on Earth. That gift and nature of mine has run through my life and may have contributed to my choices, especially in the choice of a marriage partner. It is very important to know about yourself well before you make critical life choices.

Returning to Olivier, I realized later that my 'savior's syndrome' made me love this broke man struggling at all levels. At twenty-eight years of age, he was squatting in a room in his father's house. He was tall and handsome, but these were not among the reasons why I agreed to go along with him.

The reasons why I choose to marry him were; firstly, because of his engagement to the things of God, and secondly, the fact that I was convinced that I was coming into his life to help him.

In the mind of the twenty-year-old girl I was back then, a man who was as dedicated in his church as he portrayed to be, was someone who had dedicated his life to serving Jesus Christ. Someone who was in love with the Master, just like the people I met in France who were able to spend hours in the cold in a car, just because they wanted to spend time with Jesus. I thought that love and dedication were the only motivations that could push a man to decide to serve the Master, but how wrong was I?

We started our relationship during my short stay in my home town after my second year. I spent four weeks and saw him a few times before accepting to start courting him. I traveled back to France and we started our long distance relationship. He mostly made phone calls because he was not the writing type. I still wonder how I, a lover of writing poetry, letters, and novels, was able to settle with a man who couldn't write a proper letter—the mystery of love, I assume. But was it really love or pity?

One day, as we were on the phone, he asked for my guidance on something. His father, who was not a believer, had followed a friend to visit a shrine. The occultic priest they went to meet mentioned that Olivier was struggling with his business, and he told the father that if Olivier was willing to sacrifice a goat to the deity, his business would blossom.

The truth is, he was struggling with his business. He always complained about bad sales, about people owing him money, about suppliers refusing to give him the school material in credit, or about him not being able to supply the materials to important clients like schools.

So, when I called him that evening, he asked me what I thought about sacrificing the goat. I rebuked, admonished, and told him never to consider such alternatives. I even wondered how he could give it a thought, and I rested my case, thoroughly convinced that "my" man had followed my advice and informed his father that he was uninterested. Little did I know that he went ahead and sacrificed that goat.

Truly, the fact that he asked me that question was a 'red flag', a huge warning that should have led me to call our relationship off. Still, my lack of maturity combined with my ignorance about so many things made me brush off the incident without even questioning the integrity of this so-called son of God who could consider sacrificing a goat to a deity which was not the God we served. It was like sacrificing on the devil's altar.

The man who went ahead to make the goat sacrifice was not the man I said 'yes' to a few months before. However, I did not notice the change because I was not spiritually discerning enough. I am sure that if I had paid more attention to my prayer life, the Holy Spirit would have given me a hint, but I was busy looking for menial jobs to do to earn a living. I also believe there was a specific distraction attack on my life during that season. I remember suddenly becoming addicted to the Television(TV). I had no TV set in my room and had to go to the common space to watch it, but it did not deter me from being religiously present to watch my favourite shows. I remember watching TV on a Saturday night and, as a result, missing a church service where I was supposed to sing for the first time with a new praise team. Everything was ready that Sunday, but I did not show up that Sunday morning. After that, I told them I was quitting from the singing group when they called me, and I did this just because I couldn't wake up early because of my late-night TV schedules.

I do not remember another season of my life when I approached the work of God with this kind of levity. It was very unlike me. I am usually not like that. I will never disappoint the people I have committed to. I will never miss a service on Sunday.

With all these happenings, I still did not pay attention to all these details and the obvious fact that I was waxing cold when it came to the things of God. I pursued my studies, bagged my Law Degree during the fourth year and rushed home to get married.

The second red flag was, I ignored was my mother's reluctance to my marriage with Olivier. My mother resisted the idea of this marriage with all her strength. She couldn't explain why, but I understand today that, it was God using her to stop me from making one of the biggest mistakes of my life. Praying mothers are a gift. I can tell you today that your grandmother is probably why I am still alive today. Her prayers have sustained me for almost my entire life, and I owe this woman more than I can ever repay. She refused to give my hand in marriage. One day, while trying to explain what couldn't be understood in the realm of reasoning, she mentioned that he did not have a house. The fact is, in my mother's tribe, a man had to build a house before he got married. He must at least be able to pay for the rent for his dwelling place. Olivier was staying with his father.

Instead of trying to understand her, my impression from what she said was, she despised him because he was poor. Once again, I wore my hat of 'defender of the less privileged' and started fighting my mother with all the will power I had. I put strong pressure on my mother's Pastor to convince her to let me get married. She reluctantly said yes and agreed to accept the dowry. This happened when I was still in France. The struggles with my mother had lasted for months, and the day he was told he could finally come to pay for my dowry, he called me and told me that he did not have the money to pay for the few items requested by my family. There is a little caveat here: I am not from a region where dowries cost several expensive cows and millions of any currency; my tribe prides itself in asking for only a few things to honor the parents.

He was requested to provide three 'Ankara' (wax prints) for my mother and her sister, and forty dollars equivalent in cash. I had to send him the money to pay the dowry. I was a student who sometimes slept on an empty stomach. Would you believe me if I tell you that he kept part of the money I sent and bought the cheapest type of 'Ankara' for my mother? We'll get back to that later.

So, a few months after the dowry was paid, I returned to my country to never return to Aix-en-Provence. I planned to get married, find a job, and start my life as a newly wedded wife. I was excited because the desire to get married had been in my heart since I was a teenager. Remember from my story, I always loved to attend weddings.

During the wedding preparation period, several 'red flags' were shown to me that I chose to ignore—I would pay for all of that later. One of these red flags was the fact that this man never spent a cent on me.

One of my destiny helpers was informed about my plans to get married and called my fiancée to give him an amount of money for the wedding and also to be able to secure a house for us.

Despite him having that money, he refused to give it and so, my mother and my destiny helper handled all the expenses for our wedding. At some point, I was infuriated by the fact that even the church he was, where he was an ordained worker did not do much for us. I understand now that people do not do much for people who usually do not do much for them. The worst thing was, his church members did not bring anything to the wedding, meaning they did not contribute at all but decided to manage and serve the food that had been prepared for the guests. They literally took over the serving. As a result, my family members, who practically paid for the whole wedding, and his family members, left the wedding venue on empty stomachs while his church members were sharing takeaway bags full of food. They had enough to eat and more to take home. The frustration I endured on the wedding day was just the beginning of my long journey in the den of a miserable marriage.

We started living in our small studio not far from the market where he was selling. As previously mentioned, business was not booming for him and he was blaming the whole world for it.

I felt sick a few weeks after the wedding, and when we went to the hospital, I asked for a pregnancy test because I had never felt that way in my entire life. When the results came back, boom! The excellent news came: I was pregnant. The man I married was sad when the doctor announced to us that I was pregnant. Can you believe that?

The countenance of my husband changed immediately. He became so sad that the doctor had to ask him:

- "But Sir, I understand you are married; this should be good news?"

He told the doctor that he did not expect it to happen so soon. Indeed, he had other plans. His plans were for me to find a job and, if not, to return to France and arrange his trip to join me there. I did not know he married me because he wanted to use me to satisfy his selfish desires. In his mind, I was someone with a great future who could provide for his needs; I was not meant to become a liability. A pregnancy meant that he would have to take care of me, and he never planned for that.

I was so happy. My first pregnancy. Me, the one people considered to be barren was now pregnant. My pregnancy period was a great eye-opener for me. Because it was my first pregnancy, my mother insisted that I regularly see a gynecologist. She explained that nurses can sometimes overlook details that could jeopardize my life or my baby's life. She was talking out of experience because she lost a baby before having me. When I told my husband what my mother said, his reply was, "You will consult nurses just like any other woman. If your mother wants you to see a doctor, she will have to pay for it; I do not have the money for that."

That was the end of the discussion. My mother took it upon herself to pay for my monthly consultations and scans.

Please take some time to thank your grandmother. You would have probably not been here if she had not taken me to one of the best gynaecologists of the city where we were living. He was an old man who followed up on her when she was pregnant with me.

I had monthly appointments, and she would come and pick me up even though where I was staying was about forty kilometers from her house. She will take me to the doctor and pay the consultant fees for the medical examinations, the scans, etc. The few times I asked my husband to give me some money to contribute to the hospital bills, the answer was a blunt no.

On one of these faithful days, my mother came to pick me up and dropped me off after we were done with the doctor. Before going, I asked him if he could give me the equivalent of five dollars just in case I needed to buy something for myself. He told me he did not have five dollars for me. My mother spent seventy dollars on the consultation fees, and I do not remember how much for the exams. When I returned from the clinic, my husband was not home. He came back later, after 8p.m. We sat and talked for some time about life in general then at some point, he showed me his new phone he had just bought. He was feeling very proud of himself for having been able to buy that phone. He did not notice that my countenance had changed. I became very sad. I was shocked. The same man who refused to give me five dollars that morning, was here bragging about his new phone, for which he had paid about two hundred dollars.

I started crying profusely. The pregnancy related hormones surely played a role in triggering the tears, but the major reason why I was crying was the pain I felt when I realized that the man I married was not interested in my well-being and would probably never be. I cried so much that night that he had to call his best friend and his wife to come and ask me for forgiveness. He apologized that night for ignoring my needs and only focusing on his, but he never changed, and things got even worse with time.

We moved to a new apartment when I was about six months pregnant. It was more like a room and a parlor, but was relatively cheaper than the studio. It was a better deal and we needed more space with the baby coming. I remember waking up one morning hungry. My baby probably asked for the food because I usually do not eat in the morning. I asked for a quarter of a dollar to buy some bread, but instead of giving me the money, this man started shouting at me, complaining that I was overeating. A quarter of a dollar for his pregnant wife to buy bread was just too much for him. I sat on the bed that morning, crying profusely, reminding myself that I would have never lacked any breakfast in my mother's house.

Can I tell you something, my daughter? A man who is never ready to give you anything does not love you. A genuine lover will always ensure that your needs are met and that you are satisfied. He might not be the wealthiest person on earth, but he will try his best to meet your needs within his capacity.

A few days later, I discovered a bank statement belonging to my husband. The man who denied me a quarter of a dollar a few days earlier, had almost a thousand dollars in his bank account when he told me daily that he did not have any money. I was soon going to discover that his stinginess was the least of my many problems.

There was this particular lady from the church with whom he had something doing. I mean, they were in a relationship. I once had a dream of her entering our bedroom. In the dream, I was sitting on the bed and she sat there as well and pushed me aside so that she could take my place.

A few days later, I returned from the clinic with my mother. We knocked at the apartment door and had to wait a while before the door opened. My mother and I were surprised to see this lady sitting in the living room. The apartment was small, so why it took so long for him to come and open the door, was a mystery. My mother and I entered the room and we sat there as well. The atmosphere in the room was very tense. My mother asked to take her leave after five minutes of sitting with us. Just then, the lady too asked to take her leave. When we were left alone, I tried to explain to him why a deacon serving God in a church, should not be found alone in a closed house with a young lady. He rebuked me and told me how wicked I was to throw this kind of accusation against him and someone who was supposed to be my spiritual daughter. He told me that my mind was twisted.

The following day, in church, the same lady came to meet me and told me how she was disappointed in me for having suspicion about her and my husband. I realized that he had called her and told her about our conversation. From this incident, I decided to keep things to myself.

A few months later, we discovered that the lady was pregnant. She was not married. She gave birth to a baby boy. Almost two years after the incident, she confessed publicly that she was having something with my husband. She explained that the reason why she slept with the father of her boy was the disappointment she felt after my husband dumped her. She was one of the many girls who would have an affair with this man I called my husband.

My daughter, I gave birth to you amid this chaos, but I was overjoyed. I had to move to my mother's place a few weeks before the delivery. My husband told me he did not have money to feed me. To be honest, he was not taking care of any of my needs. All my pregnancy clothes were gifts from my mother. She was the one giving me money for almost everything. I would stay with my hair unkept for weeks until I visited my family. My mother, in the pretense of paying for my transportation, would give me money to cater for my needs. She could see that I was neglected, but she never said anything. She never reminded me that she warned me against this man who was insisting on marrying me almost as if his life depended on it. This same man ended up treating me like a non-entity.

Your father would send me back to my mother's place at the least opportunity, because he did not have money to take care of me. The first two years of that sham of marriage were hellish, because Olivier made me pay for the fact I had become a liability and not the cash cow that he was expecting me to have been.

I cannot count the number of nights I woke up crying, asking myself if that was the end of everything. I cannot say what was going through his mind, but my interpretation of the situation was that he never loved me but rather, saw in me a girl with a lot of potential who would help him out of poverty. Marrying me was his ticket out of his world of lack. Unfortunately for him and me, I was the one he needed to support, at least for the first years of our marriage, and he wanted to make me pay for it. I lost count of the humiliations similar to the event I just narrated. Young ladies from the church or friends of his would come and confront me or humiliate me. People were openly mocking me. I was a shadow of myself, hardly having what was required to cater to my needs.

I remember the visit of one of his old friends. They reconnected, but I do not know how, and she came to visit him. I could see the despise in her eyes. I was sitting outside on the stairs. She did not know anything about me. She did not know I had a master's in Business and Corporate law. She did not know I was fluent in both French and English. All she saw was a lady who was not as classy as she was. I remember wearing a white linen top and blue striped pants. I was a mother of one without any money to make my hair. I had no make-up because I never liked make-up. She was dressed to impress, and she did not meet her match. I overheard their conversation when she asked him why he did not marry her, implying she had more to offer than me. He replied that he did not know she had feelings for him. They were giggling, smiling, laughing while my heart was bleeding.

She left after a few hours. They were in my living room, while I was sitting in my kitchen all alone. For months, your father will be screaming her name occasionally. He even explained that she was from a rich family and had a great job. It was obvious that he felt he settled for the wrong horse. I was not bringing in anything to contribute to the home. During the first months of our marriage, he pressured me to go and ask for money from my family to pay for our rent. I refused vehemently and told him it was unthinkable from where I came from. I guess the humiliations I was enduring from him were my punishment for not cooperating in trying to deprive my mother of her hard-earned money.

Anytime I tell the story of my marriage, people ask me why I did not leave earlier, why I chose to endure so many humiliations at the hands of a man who did not love me. I told you about my admiration for Abigail in the Bible because she did not allow Nabal's wickedness to affect her. I say it because I know how this marriage badly affected my soul. The joyful girl who met this man a few years back had turned into a sorrowful woman who couldn't remember what laughter was. I was sad all day. I was weeping all night for close to two good years.

The humiliation was coming from the fact that I was not earning anything. It became so bad that I started looking for a job during my pregnancy. Of course, nobody will hire a pregnant woman. After giving birth to you my daughter, I decided to return to school to earn another degree. Once again, my mother paid for the courses and took care of you when I ran to take those classes. She would be taking care of you until I was back from my classes to breastfeed you. I was spending most of my time at her place. Our tradition requires an experienced mother to take care of a newborn. Ideally, one of your grandmothers should have moved in with us, but we had only one bedroom, so the best option was to stay with her. Those days at your grandmother's place were times of refreshment for me. I could eat to my satisfaction; I had people to help me to take care of you. I could rest.

When you were three months old, your father asked me to come and visit him every weekend to attend church service. One of these Sundays, he told me to get you ready to go and visit his mother. We went there and something happened that, I will never forget and was never able to forgive your father for.

His mother prepared a concoction—I did not know it was for you. All of a sudden, she had people from her household hold you and force you to open your mouth. She spat on the herbs she was squeezing in her hands and put them in your mouth.

I felt like dying. I couldn't shout; I couldn't defend you, but the expression on my face showed so much anger that one of your aunties from your father's side took me to her room to appease me. I was furious. How did this Pastor let this happen to my child? How could he allow someone to spit into your mouth? When they were done, you were crying so much that they brought you back to me to breastfeed you. I never allowed anyone else to touch you after that.

When we got home, this man had the nerve to tell me that it was a treatment because you were too big and that, his mother thought that you needed it to improve your breathing. I was out of control. I told him the next time he would set me up to have someone spit in the mouth of my child, would be the day he would discover who I was. He blamed me for not believing in African medicines. I told him I had nothing against it, but any concoction made with saliva could never be good because of the lack of hygiene. Besides, what I did not understand was why his mother did not ask for my saliva or his saliva and decided that her saliva was the right choice to enter my child's mouth. A line was crossed that day, and things never improved after that despicable act. I saw a spiritual meaning to it while they were trying to convince me that it was just a traditional treatment. This was my first real fight with your father, and I remember him telling me that he never knew I could react that way.

Three weeks after that so-called treatment, while we were back at my mother's place, you had an attack in the middle of the night. You shouted like never before. It was about three in the morning, and everybody was sleeping. You were struggling to breathe and even defecated on yourself out of distress. I called an excellent friend of mine who was studying medicine. She told me to go to the teaching hospital in Cocody because they had the best pediatricians. We rushed there with your grandmother. The doctor told us that you urgently needed oxygen. She recommended that we put you in a separate room because you were so young that you could get an infection if admitted to a common room with other patients. I had nothing in terms of money. Once again, your grandmother stepped in for me. We took a room where you were admitted for six long days, with doctors trying to understand what had happened to you. They tried the strongest antibiotics they could use on a child of your age to stabilize you. Your grandmother and I were praying for you not to die, and thanks to the One who was with me in that pit of a marriage, you did not die.

Your father crossed another line during that trying week in the hospital. People came from everywhere to visit us. Your father was barely there, but his friends, church members, and colleagues from the market came. Nobody gave us a cent, and my mother had to take care of all the bills and the prescriptions. On the fourth day in the hospital, a group of youth from the church came to visit, and they told me what your father was telling me. He told his church members that he would not spend a cent on you in the hospital because I refused to use the concoction that his mother recommended that could have helped to prevent the issue. I was shocked; I did not show it to the people narrating what your father said; I just kept it to myself. I think I never forgave your father for that statement and for the fact that, he would have watched you die only to make a point.

On the day of our discharge from the hospital, there was the remaining bill of about a hundred and twenty dollars. I begged him to take care of it because I heard his colleagues and friends had contributed some money and given it to him to take care of the child. He refused to pay the bill, and this act confirmed to me that he had indeed uttered this awful statement.

Chapter Six

HE NEVER FORSAKES, NEVER ABANDONS

Your father never wanted to spend a dime on me or any of his children with me. You were his firstborn (at least from what I know). The day you were born, I called him on my way to the hospital. It was eight in the morning, you were born at 10am, and your father showed up at the hospital at 4pm in the afternoon. I do not know why he was not hurrying up to meet you considering the fact that you were the first one that opened the womb. He came when everything was done, and I was about to be discharged. My mother had already paid all the hospital bills by the time he came. I asked him to reimburse her, but he never did. It was a public hospital, and the bill was nothing out of reach for the average man. Mechanics, Drivers, and Cooks were paying the same fees. Some patients were even paying more because they underwent caesarean sections. I did not have a caesarean section. His excuse was, he did not have the money. It was just an equivalent of twenty dollars for a pregnancy that lasted nine months, and for which he never paid for the doctor's consultations. Remember, even during the pregnancy, he refused to buy bread for me to eat. He could not save twenty dollars from the hundreds of dollars he had and I had seen from his bank statement only three months before. Knowing your father as I know him now, I am convinced he had that money, but he just decided not to spend a dime on me and my baby.

It was the same story when I had your brother almost two years after you. He told me he had no money to pay the hospital bills. It was also a public hospital. All he had to pay was twenty-four dollars this time. I was making a small amount of money then from my job. I paid all the bills that time and I was glad I did. At least, I did not have to face the shame of having my mother pay the bills again for my second pregnancy when I was legally married.

I was gainfully employed by the time I was pregnant the third time. My job paid quite well when your sister was born. Interestingly, something happened during the time I was pregnant. I gave eight hundred dollars to your father to deposit for me in my personal bank account. I was quite busy and had no time to do it myself. I was working, I had money and wanted to be in excellent condition for my third child. I planned to give birth in a private hospital. My gynecologist asked for five hundred dollars for his fees in the private hospital. I was therefore getting ready for what he required, but also to buy other needs such as diapers, cologne, powder, baby articles of clothing, etc...

I gave your father the money to deposit into my bank account during the seventh month of the pregnancy. A few days later, I asked him to give me the receipt from the bank, and he started yelling that I did not trust him. About two weeks later, I noticed someone was calling him repeatedly, but he was not answering. It was obvious that something was bothering him. He was no longer eating and was losing weight.

This happened at a time when we were married for almost six years, and God had helped me with my career through His mercies. I was making about a thousand five hundred dollars per month. I had money to take care of things at home. We had moved to a better house, in a choice area closer to my new office.

I asked him what was going on and he told me how he had borrowed eight hundred dollars from a lady, and added it to the eight hundred dollars I gave him to deposit for me, and added four hundred dollars of his own money, to invest in a deal that had failed. What was the deal? People had contacted him to tell him about how to clean money with chemicals. He showed me the papers, which were fake documents from an organization that they claimed was affiliated with the one I was working for. He gave a whopping two thousand dollars to someone who vanished into thin air, and here he was being harassed by the lady from whom he had borrowed the money. I was dumbfounded. All he had to do to avoid this unfortunate event was to ask me if the letter they gave to him months before they took the money from him was an original. But he did not. He was greedy and had plans for the millions he thought he would make. These plans did not involve his family, so I was not supposed to know. At the end of the day, because he was my husband, I had to pay the lady and forget about the money I thought I had saved to pay my hospital bills. It was just like a goodbye kiss to my money.

The day I was to deliver your brother, I had exactly five hundred dollars on me, which was exactly the amount the doctor required, but I needed extra money to pay for the required hygiene products. I made a stop at the chemist on my way to the hospital. Your father was following me closely. I wanted to buy the biggest size of cologne and powder, then he started complaining. I told him that the baby was coming to stay and that the biggest size was the best option to choose in order to save money. I was hoping he would add up to the money left to pay for the hospital bill. After all, I had seen an exchange between him and his longtime girlfriend, Suzan, a few weeks before. She was asking him for money. I was heavily pregnant then, and I cried my eyes out when I saw this. I was hoping that Suzan was in the past.

Back to my delivery at the private hospital, I had the baby around 2am. In the morning, I gave him four hundred dollars and asked him to top up the remaining hundred dollars. He once again told me that he did not have a cent. I had to borrow money from a colleague to pay the doctor and the hospital in full. I had to borrow money because your brother was born on the thirteenth, and I was paid on the seventeenth.

The interesting aspect of the issue was that, my office paid its employees a spousal allowance. Your father received the equivalent of my monthly salary as his own spouse allowance. I requested for all that allowance that was in arrears.

So, because it was a spouse allowance, I decided to give the entire money to him. I had never been the greedy, selfish type and would never be. I only asked if he could pay the hundred dollars I borrowed from my colleague to contribute to the hospital bills for at least one of his children. Guess what? The answer was a blunt "no." If I needed evidence that this man had vowed never to take care of me and my children, I had it that day when he was standing before me, with his hands full of the money I had just given him. He had one thousand four hundred dollars, all he was to do was, he was supposed to deduct a hundred dollars to help pay for the fees incurred to deliver his third child. He told me he had plans for the money. I looked at him in total disbelief and did not utter a word. After all, when a man does not love you, he will never give anything to you. Three children were delivered in the hospital without my so-called husband paying a dime for hospital consultations and delivery. That was my story as a married woman. I had made that choice of marrying him, so I was dealing with it.

I am telling you all this to help you understand how hellish a marriage can be when you end up with the wrong person.

Talking about hell, I briefly mentioned Suzan earlier, let me explain who she was in a few lines.

When you were ten months old, one of my destiny helpers, who wanted to help me again, asked me to start working for her. She was paying me daily an amount that was to be used for my transportation, but the money was helping me a lot to take care of you as well. Because I was leaving the house in the morning and was coming back home around six in the evening, I needed someone to take care of you. Your father suggested someone he knew. A young lady who was just eighteen or nineteen years old. The day she came, I interviewed her, and she told me she had never been to school. I pitied that girl and told myself I would help her when things got better for me. In the meantime, we agreed on a salary for her to take care of you. After a few weeks, I was able to secure a new job in a company. I was making a hundred dollars more than my benefactor gave me, so she happily released me to take the new job. I started working there in September and used part of my first salary to organize a small party for your first birthday in October. Suzan was helping with organizing the party. She did something wrong that day and I scolded her. Your father became furious and abused me like never before just because I had scolded her.

I was in shock, but this was just the beginning. After a few weeks of her working for us, I noticed that anytime I reached the house, she was already bathed, smelt fresh, was well-dressed and looked rosy ready to go back to her house. The girl who used to come with big t-shirts and long skirts suddenly turned into a model, wearing skimpy and revealing clothes. As soon as I reached the house, she would hand you over to me and leave, followed by your father, who would go along with her, leaving you and me alone.

This continued for a few weeks. He would come back around ten or sometimes 12pm at night. I asked him one day why he was following our house help and leaving me alone after a long day in the office. He told me he was following her because they were going in the same direction. This behavior of his was creating a lot of tension between us.

I remember one time when she left your clothes soaked in a bucket of water for two days in our bathroom. That night, I returned from the office, and she left alone this time because your father had visitors. I greeted them, entered our single bedroom, and came out to shower after a long workday. Because of the apartment's configuration, I had to cross the living room where the visitors were sitting to reach the bathroom. I went, took my shower, and came out. On my way back to the bedroom to dress up, I was stopped by your father, who started yelling at me because I was the laziest person he had ever met. He was complaining about the fact that I had left the clothes of my child soaked in a bucket for two days. I was in shock. I asked him why he did not yell at the person who left the clothes in the water in the first place. His response was even more astonishing: "I did not want to scold her in front of people."

Yet, here he was yelling at me, his wife, his child's mother in front of the same visitors. Suzan had the respect I never had from him. The emotional abuse I was going through was of the highest intensity. He never missed an opportunity to tell me how wonderful she was and how useless I was. She was a better cook; she cared for my child better than I did. Every day, he reminded me that she was this and she was that.

He never missed an occasion to tell me that I was not beautiful, and that he married me because I was smart and not because he was attracted to me. This man destroyed my already fragile self-esteem. I grew up in a family of beautiful girls and ladies, and I was likened to the black swan among them. The conversations and statements I heard from adults in my family growing up had robbed me of my confidence. I will never forget the statement of one of my numerous uncles when he saw me for the first time. He asked my mother and his sister:

> "Is that your daughter? How can a beautiful woman like you give birth to a girl like that?"

This statement summarizes well what I had to endure growing up just because I looked like my father and not like my gorgeous mother. Years later, the man I married will repeat these statements by reminding me of how ugly I was according to him and my family members.

Somehow, instead of these statements breaking me, these words helped me to focus on developing what I believed would be the only way to make it in life: My brain. I was not beautiful according to them, so I would try my best to be brilliant.

Back to Suzan, I insisted on sending her away because I was no more comfortable with the treatment I was receiving from your father because of her. He never treated me well in the first place, but her coming to be our house helped worsened things. I paid her salary, but your father forbade me to send her away.

So I endured living with her. Eventually, something happened that I couldn't stand again. One Sunday after church, we sat in the small restaurant next to the church building to have some local food. She was carrying you on her lap, sitting on the table with me and a friend of your father.

One of her acquaintances, a young man in his twenties, came to speak with her. At some point, he moved his mouth closer and closer to hers, and I had to stop him because my son was on her lap. I asked the young man to give the adults sitting at the table the required respect. He left, and this case was finished in my opinion. I did not tell Suzan anything again regarding this incident and moved on with my life. After all, she was not the one bringing her mouth closer to the young man's.

A few hours after the incident, I received a lecture from my "dear" husband about how bad a wife I was. He claimed I was the kind of woman that chased souls from the kingdom because of how I spoke to them. The kind of woman that spoke rudely to a young man who would never become a church member just because of me.

I was mortified. To tell you how I did not hold any grudge against Suzan, I never thought for a second that she could be the one who had narrated the story in such a biased manner to my husband. My mind went to your father's friend, and the following Tuesday, while the service was going on in church, I asked him for a few minutes of his time to settle the issue. I was fuming inside all this while. Thank God for self-mastery. I politely asked him if he told my husband that I disrespectfully scolded the young man. He said no and added that he supported my gesture that day because he also felt the young man lacked manners. That was it. I suddenly realized that Suzan was the one who had told the biased story to your father.

I went straight to her house. You were on my back, and I was three months pregnant with your brother. As usual, she pretended to be the nicest person on earth. I do not know how people can become so evil at a very young age. I spoke with her gently, advised her about the need to be closer to the woman of the house as a house help. I gave her the salary I owed her that month and asked her not to return to my house the following day.

Just ten minutes after our conversation, just as I was standing at the table of a fruit seller I knew, asking if her sister could come and take care of you the following day because I had to go to work, your father stormed out of the church and started insulting me. He was the one preaching that day, but he dropped the microphone and left the altar when Susan called him. He stopped everything to come and find me on that road where dozens of people were watching him abusing me: He raved,

"You are just a whore, nothing but a whore. Who do you think you are to chase her from the house? Whether you like it or not, she will return tomorrow, and nothing will stop her. It's my house, and you are not making the decision."

People were begging him to stop talking and were asking him to solve whatever issue it was in our home peacefully, but he went on ranting. I was quiet, too ashamed to utter a word.

I entered a taxi to go to the house and called the Pastor. He came that night with his wife, and they decided on Suzan's case. It was agreed that she was no longer allowed in the house. That never stopped your father from seeing her. Church members started calling my attention to the fact that my so-called husband was spending hours at her place (it was not far from the church). He was coming back home around midnight. When I confronted him about it, he beat the hell out of me despite knowing that I was pregnant. I was in a messy marriage situation.

I was crying so much during that time that I realised I was becoming bitter. In that situation, my first Lover reminded me of His unconditional love for me again. I was so down, and one day, I heard Him say:

"Be careful; bitterness is settling into your heart, and this will lead to your spiritual death. Once you are spiritually dead, your physical death will follow."

My God, this warning hit me hard, and I made up my mind never to allow this man's actions to hurt me anymore. I resolved in my heart not to be moved even if I found him sleeping on our bed with a woman. It was not easy, but I was motivated by the fact that I did not want to die. Who would take care of my children? I couldn't afford to die.

Suzan remained in the life of your father as his girlfriend until I left him. He was just in love with her. Over the years, he used the money I was bringing home to set up businesses for her and rent an apartment for her too. He probably thinks I did not know, but people who were so appalled and disgusted by the situation that they were coming to me to report these incidents, hoping that I would react. I never reacted. I was silent, and I put a barricade around my heart to prevent hatred and anger from entering. It was too costly to be bitter; I just could not afford it.

Comfort and solace, as I already explained, came from my professional life. I started a new job just before you were a year old. By the time your brother was six months old, I got another job with an organization which gave me five times my previous salary. When your sister clocked one, I got promoted to an international position that gave me five times what I was making in the local capacity. Because he needed the money I was making, your father started giving me some respect; at least, he pretended to do so. There was no more abuse for me. After all, I was the breadwinner, and he couldn't afford to upset me. During this time, your father squandered my hard-earned money. Once again, I was never stingy. I never made him pay for what he did to me when I was lacking financially. He had access to my bank accounts and even emptied one to buy himself a luxury car unknown to me. When I got to know it, I decided to close my eyes once again, for peace sake and to retain my sanity. I endured other humiliations. Your father was sleeping with the maids I hired to take care of you and your brothers. He was like a possessed man. A deacon serving God zealously in the church, what an irony! But was he a Child of God? Someone who had sacrificed to another deity than Jehovah God. Someone who was reluctantly praying or meditating on the word of God? Someone who admitted that he was struggling to pay his tithes. I realized too late that I was unequally yoked with someone from the kingdom of darkness who pretended to be a child of light.

One day, your father did something that ended up as the straw that broke the camel's back. It was nothing compared to the other things he had done, but my resistance level had significantly reduced. I was worn out. I was on a mission in a country not far from our home country. He traveled to visit me for a week, and I discovered on the last day of his stay that he had travelled with a girlfriend to my station. I do not know if it was Suzan or someone else. But that day, right at the bus station, I discovered that he had plans other than to return to the children. After leaving him, I decided I would never be available for this relationship again. Enough was enough. What scared me the most were the sexual diseases that I could have gotten in this marriage. I remember asking for a full medical analysis each time I was pregnant, including a test for HIV. My gynecologist, who was a Muslim one day, asked me why I was systematically asking for an HIV test when I was with a husband who was a devout Christian. I couldn't reply. Yet deep down within me, I was terrified. I knew he was not taking any precautions with his loose sexual life, so yes, my life was at risk.

After he left, he called me several times, but I refused to pick up his calls. I cried my eyes out once again and then went to God in prayers, asking Him for permission to leave the marriage. I was tired of being treated like trash. The fact that my so-called husband couldn't travel for a week without a mistress was too much for me.

The following day, someone called my mother and gave her a message from God for me. The message was "He, God had granted me the permission I had requested." The person did not know what I asked permission for. The only message she gave my mother was:

"God said you should tell your daughter that she has the permission she asked for."

That was the day of my deliverance. The prayer was made in a room where I was alone, thousands of kilometers away from my family. I had said nothing to my mother or anyone else. The tears I cried that day were to my first Lover asking Him if I could, despite being a Christian, leave a marriage that was destroying me.

His answer was "Yes," and that's how I started separating from your father and finally asking for a divorce.

Chapter Seven

HE ANSWERS WHEN I CALL, AND HE IS MY DELIVERER

Sometimes, I wonder if I have been healed from the trauma I went through during that period of my life. I had almost ten years of humiliation and hurts, during which time my only way of escape/ solace and comfort was my relationship with my First Lover, by now you know who that is, He is Jesus Christ.

He was the one I cried to because none of my tears ever moved your father. He was the One I spoke to because your father never had time to listen to me; he was the One bringing me the joy, the comfort, and the hope I needed to keep living because your father never showed me that he cared.

You will probably be in shock if I tell you I am grateful to God for that portion of my journey. I am grateful for the lessons I learnt, grateful because these trials were not able to overcome me, but they have certainly shaped me into a better version of myself. The objective of my enemy was to kill me or at least kill my dreams through that dire process, but I came out alive with so many lessons.

These are lessons that I can boldly share with the world today to open the eyes of many and stop them from making the mistakes I made.

One lesson I will never forget is related to the interpretation of a revelation someone received from God. A few days after your father sacrificed the goat to the shrine he visited with his father, I have mentioned this earlier on in my narrative, he had a dream he narrated to me

In the dream, your father's business was depleting until he became wretched. In the same dream, I was prospering, making a lot of money. The dream came when we were engaged to be married. The interpretation he got from people in his church was that, I was a supposedly witch who had come to destroy his life. He was warned to be careful about me. Nobody understood that it was a warning from God asking your father to repent of his sinful ways. For years, I would try my best to debunk these interpretation targeting me. A few days before I decided to leave your father, while we were together during his infamous stay to visit me, he mentioned to me that had had another dream similar to the one he had years earlier. This time, the people he explained his dream to, told him I would leave our home and he would find himself in a very abject poverty. The truth is at this point, his business was already inexistent and I was the one sponsoring his lavish lifestyle, including the several girlfriends he was impressing with my hard-earned money. When the second revelation came, he boldly told people that he could bet his life on it by putting his hand in the fire if need be because, he was sure I could never leave him.

He had made me go through hell for years, and I was still there, so he was confident in the fact that I was stuck with him despite all he was doing. This conversation happened a few days before I made up my mind to leave him, and a few months before our divorce. He was boasting to me about that conversation, not knowing that it would be over between us in few days' time. My guess is that, he understood that these dreams were God's warning, but he just brushed it off as usual. Your father never had any regard for God's warnings. I am sure he had several of them in the course of time that he was sleeping with the maids and girls from the church, but he never really showed that he cared about them.

A huge lesson I learnt is, never follow a man who cannot obey God. I already mentioned the importance of getting married to a man who can hear God, but now I would like to dwell on the need to ensure that the man you are getting married to follows God's instructions and yields to them wholeheartedly. I have been a first-hand victim of a man who does not follow God's guidance. Obedience, the Bible says, is better than sacrifice; my own experience is that sacrifice, by obedience is the best way to go. Abraham sacrificed Isaac by obedience, and this act touched God. Men who have mastered the art of combining obedience with sacrifice will be sought after. I was married to a man who was not obedient to God; if not, he would have stopped living as an adulterer. Besides, the word sacrifice seemed to be unknown to your father. He admitted several times, even in public, that he struggled to give to God. The only person who mattered to your father was himself. I remember buying a gift for his father the first time I met him. The old man later told me that it was the only gift he had ever presented to him.

Another important lesson from my sad story is this, please pay close attention to how the man you want to marry treats his family members, especially his sisters if he has any. Your father had an elder sister who practically raised him, but he never gifted her anything, even when he was enjoying the money he was taking from me. A man like your father, who never gave a gift to someone who was like his mother, will probably never give anything to his wife when he finally gets married. Pay close attention to such details, and believe me when I tell you that it matters.

I also want to acknowledge my part and my responsibility for the failed relationship. I was far from perfect.

My first mistake was not seeking God's whole counsel before committing to something as important as marriage. Please never make such a decision in seasons when your spiritual life is down. You need to ensure that you prayerfully enquire from God about who to marry, when to marry, and when it comes to other important life decisions, ask God first. Another important aspect to inquire from God is the vision of the man you are planning to marry. A man can indeed be in the will of God for your life, but if he is visionless, he will mislead you.

Many Christians do not know that God speaks, or realize that God is so interested in providing and is ready to provide the needed guidance. He remains Abba, our Father. How can a good father be watching silently when his child is going to fall into a trap? I can assure you that while you are walking towards the hole or trap, our Father God will be speaking. He keeps warning us. The main issue is when we become insensitive to His voice and cannot hear Him. We need to become familiar with His voice and His way of saying things. For that to happen, we need to train ourselves to hear Him.

Prayer is the main communication tool when relating with God; just like any communication mechanism, it is a two-way affair. We speak to God, and God speaks to us. A prayer life without hearing God is not ideal, and that's why prayer should be combined with the meditation of the Word. God's primary way of communicating with us is through His Word.

Another critical point is the need to tarry until we hear God's voice. The new generation of Christians do not have the required patience to wait until the Lord speaks. Our time is so much solicited by social media and other things, we want or need to attend to such that that we try to make the time with God as brief as possible. The issue is, if you do not tarry, you will not hear from Him. God is God, and He speaks to us according to His terms and in His time. He will not yield to the pressure of a man who thinks he is in a hurry while he is not really going anywhere.

Another element is the need to be still before hearing from God. There is so much noise around and inside us nowadays that, we can barely hear God. Most of the noise to me, comes from social media. It is a colossal distraction that might destroy an entire generation if we are not careful. The noise can also come from our minds. When we are unsettled, our minds produce a lot of noise out of fear and anxiety. That's why peace is so important.

My second mistake was, not listening to my mother when she did not agree with this relationship. I mentioned earlier that praying parents are a gift, and when they provide guidance, it is wise to follow it. Good parents will always have good intentions for their children, so if and when they ask you to be careful, do not credit them with bad ones. Ask yourself, why can someone who has been nothing but good to me all my life suddenly change? Also, you probably know your parents better than the new character recently introduced in your life's plot. You do not know his intentions, but the intention of your parents are certainly for good and not for evil.

My third mistake was probably the fact that, I allowed myself to be manipulated by a narcissist who only cared about himself. I gave him everything he asked for. At some point, I wanted to buy his love. I was sponsoring his lavish lifestyle by buying him expensive gifts I did not buy for myself. He had the latest gadgets, phones, tablets, and cars. How many times did he manipulate me to invest in his so-called ventures? He wanted to start a company, and to do that, he needed to buy a property. I gave him eight thousand dollars from my hard-earned money. At some point, this man who denied me a piece of bread when I was pregnant for him was driving three luxury cars entirely paid for by me. The funny thing is, he had his name on all the papers of these cars. I paid for them, but they never belonged to me. The day I signed the contract to buy a house in my name, he left the office of the Estate Builders Company in a lot of fury. Why did I dare buy a house in my name? When I asked for a divorce, he started approaching a few of my friends to beg me to come back. All he kept saying was related to the house I was building, and how I wanted to deprive him of living in it after all the years of scarcity, we had spent together.

When I narrated my story during the divorce proceedings, the judge asked him if what I said was true. And he couldn't lie that day. Thanks be to God for that. The judge then turned to me and wanted to know why I had stayed so long in such a hellish marriage even though my life was at stake. After admitting all the horrors he took me through, he had the guts to tell the judge that the house I was building, and the land I bought in another city (which I had forgotten about) were not mentioned in the agreement we signed. He wanted a fair share of my landed properties even though the deal prepared by my lawyers following my instructions, left him with the cars and other items in the house I had purchased over the years. He was still, fighting to have a share of my landed properties, knowing fully well that he never contributed a dime to any of the things "we" had.

The judge did not bother to respond to his question. She saw him for who he was: A predator who was obviously preying on me. A parasite who was sucking, swallowing, spending, and squandering the money I was working hard to make from a job that was taking me to the most challenging places where he couldn't have survived for even an hour. I was working hard, and sometimes trekking under the harsh sun for hours. The average temperature in one of the localities I worked at was about 45 degrees Celsius. I remember how we struggled with water shortage for months in some places. The funny part is, he never had the time to even listen to the predicament I was going through when I bothered to share them with him. I remember calling him after a difficult day at work. I was facing challenges and I needed someone to pray for me. His only reaction was to shout at me and tell me to make sure I kept my job. Once again, my mother listened to me and prayed for me. I learnt years later that, she never ceased to pray for me. She knew I was miserable in that marriage; she supported me as best as she could, but she never uttered a single word to remind me that she warned me not to go into that marriage. I pray to have the same kind of wisdom and be there silently supporting others in challenging times because sometimes, speaking will do more harm than good. Please, my daughter, I beg you never to marry a lazy man or worse, a lazy narcissist.

How do you recognize them?

- They do not work hard and often come up with excuses about why they are failing in their field of endeavors. No man can succeed without the hard work and the help of God, obtained through prayer and the study of the Word. I begged your father several times to go for a retreat because I knew his prayerless life was the reason behind his struggles. Once, I even paid for him to go and lodge somewhere for a retreat. A few days later, when I called, I realized he had gone to stay at the place of a friend who was an unbeliever. That's what he told me, but he did not know that I knew that his friend was staying a few blocks from the apartment he was renting for Suzan. He was probably staying at Suzan's place instead of going for a retreat, which possibly could have saved his destiny. When I heard him later complaining about the fact that I wrecked his destiny, I felt like laughing. The truth is, no man's destiny is in the hands of another man

The only Maker of destinies is Jehovah God. So, for a man to fulfill destiny, he needs to be close to the Maker. In the words of a renowned Man of God, "Every man is responsible for the outcome of his life."

• You recognize narcissist's from the way they blame others and never assume responsibility for their failures or mistakes. A man who can never admit that he played a role in whatever is happening in his life is unreliable.

• They can do anything to obtain things for themselves, including lying and manipulating others.

-God and others are never the priority in their lives. Their selfish self is their only priority. It's always about them—what they can get and what they can do. Selfishness and self-centeredness are killing so many marriages today.

I already spoke about the 'kings in the making.' Kings in the Kingdom we operate in, are never self-centred because God prepares them to care for people. Servant leaders are men with hearts who can sacrifice everything for their families' well-being and the people in their care in general. The drive to find a solution to the plight of others is often the criteria God uses to lift people. Selfish people can rise, but they usually have to require the support of other spiritual entities.

Abraham cared for Lot even after his nephew showed the highest disrespect for him. He couldn't just let Lot die in the hands of the enemy. Joseph, genuinely cared for his brothers, and Moses was a great leader because he passionately cared for the people of Israel. David learned it while caring for the sheep of his father. Jesus cared for us to the point that, He accepted to lay down His life for us. If you do not see genuine care in a man's attitude and words, please run away from such a man.

My last mistake was allowing anger to settle in my heart. While ensuring I was not becoming bitter, I did not realize that anger was quietly taking over. Anger was a family issue from my father's side. I was exposed to it at a tender age, when I witnessed fights between my father and his brother. I cannot tell why they were fighting, but I can never forget the fury in the room and the knives they were using to threaten themselves. My father was known for his anger. Anger used the challenges in my marriage to have a grip on me, and I did not realize it then until years later, when I started reacting by yelling at people for next to nothing. I was yelling at my children, colleagues, and friends. I was flaring up for insignificant issues. The Holy Spirit pointed it to me, and we worked together to fix the problem. I know anger is still looking for the slightest opportunity to come back and rear its head in my life. Still, I thank God for the fact that some of my reactions, such as yelling, are no more, but I still react sharply sometimes, especially when I am confronted with what I consider to be disrespect or injustice. I am still in the process of learning how to act and not to react.

I will end this chapter by stating a few things I praise myself for, and I'm grateful to God for, in these rough times I spent in the hands of a man who is like my enemy because of the way he treated me.

I will probably shock you, but the first thing I will mention here is that, I had this man's back and his interests at heart despite all he did. I believe God helped me to remain a supportive wife despite through it all because He did not want to have a case against me in the Court of Heaven. I can count the number of times I disrespected the man I married. I gave him all the honor I could, I went as far as defending him when people accused him of things I knew he did. But I stood by him because I saw it as my role as a wife. I guess some eyes are rolling already from disbelief, and I fully understand that but I think you can disapprove of someone's acts and still stand by them because it is your duty. I stood by this horrible man through thick and thin, and I believe that's the reason why God had my back all through this terrible time. I think that's why my voice crying out for vengeance could be heard in the court of heaven and is still being heard today. This man cannot do anything against me because he does not have a case against me. I even left him without exposing him. I could have messed up his life by telling everyone what he did to me, but I chose to keep it a secret.

The day before we met in court for the divorce hearing, a delegation from his church authorities came to my mother's place. I refused to meet them because I did not want to tell them why I was leaving this man. Until today, he is going about telling people I dumped him because I became rich. He did that in a bid to destroy my reputation. He did that because I took the stand not to tell people then who he really was. I am sure that my God is avenging me because I did not avenge for myself. I also believe God is defending me because I did not defend myself. And to the people who believed that I was a witch sent to destroy the destiny of this man, I want to ask you a few questions:

Why is God punishing him and not the supposed witch? Why is God lifting the supposed witch and not the 'devoted deacon who claims he was a victim?' Is God unfair, or is He allowing the devil to have the final say by lifting a 'so-called Jezebel' like you claim I was? I beg you all to please go and pray, and learn the ways of the Lord. The God I serve is the Lifter of Men, I believe He is the One who is lifting me, blessing me, and protecting my children and me. The God that this man pretends to serve should have lifted him and not afflicted him with all the trouble he went through.

The other thing I will praise myself and God for is the fact that, this marriage did not change me to become the worst version of myself. Anger indeed settled in, but I thank God for keeping the essence of the virtues he gave me for my journey on Earth. I said compassion and empathy are two of my essential tools as a helper. Being manipulated by a man such as Olivier could have turned me into someone who refuses to help others, but my God did not allow it to happen. One virtue I almost lost in the process is joy, but in recent years, God has been insistent about me regaining it. The things that happened to me deeply hurt my soul, and I am still fighting to have my joy restored perfectly just like Jesus wants me to have, but I am rest assured that I am progressively getting there.

I can never thank Jesus Christ, my First Lover enough for staying in the pit with me all these year, and for rescuing me from the pit when enough was enough, and for eventually leading me unto the restoration path.

Let's now move to the restoration pathway.

Part Three

DIVORCED BUT NOT REJECTED

Chapter Eight

HE RESTORES AND GIVES ME BEAUTY FOR ASHES

I want to thank God for being with me in Court and through the divorce proceedings. Of course, this man did not want to let go of the 'milky cow.' He was begging, talking to my friends, sending delegations to my mother's house to dissuade me from proceeding with the divorce, but the Lord helped me.

The Holy Spirit instructed me to pray in tongues, and I was deep in prayer while this man was signing the agreement prepared by my lawyers. He signed everything in front of me in the courthouse. He was insulting me through the process but there was an unseen power pushing him to sign the documents. I know my Heavenly Father was at work, and I am marveled at how He helped me.

My God gave me favor with my lawyer and the judge who empathized with me, especially after the man acknowledged that all I narrated was true. I believe that truth should be the trademark of genuine children of God. Lies are from the devil, and anytime we give ourselves to lies, we are surrendering our lives to the devil, who is the father of all lies. I did not add anything to the story or cook up any lie to draw anybody's sympathy. I tried my best to provide the details I remembered, and my story touched everybody, including the judge. Her question to me was:

"Why did you stay that long? Did you want to die?"

I told her that as a Christian, I never envisaged divorce as an option, but then it became too much to bear.

Custody of the children became an issue. He wanted to keep them because if he had them, he would receive money from me to sponsor his lifestyle and continue his relationships with people he loved, such as Suzan and the people he was giving his money to instead of taking from them.

My children stayed with him for almost a year and a half. I call them my children because he was never a father to you and your brothers. A father is a provider, someone who cares about the well-being of his children. Your father never cared for you much. During the months you stayed with him, I was sending large amounts of money, roughly five thousand dollars a month to pay for rent, food, nannies, fuel, school fees, etc. One day, I received a call from him informing me the fact that your brother had fainted in school because of hunger. He had the nerve to complain about the fact that your brother was picky about food. What happened was, your father wouldn't buy attieke for your brother to eat from time to time. The nannies explained to me that the only food available in the house was rice because I would buy bags of rice anytime I would come to visit. So instead of giving money for them to buy varieties of food for his own children, this man will tell the nannies to cook rice which I brought. One day, your brother decided to stop eating and that's how come he fainted in school.

When this man called me to complain about a six-year-old boy who was too picky with food, I restrained myself from asking him why he couldn't just buy the 'attieke' for him? How much does this food cost? It costs next to nothing. Instead of responding,, I kept silent and vowed to myself that I would by all means possible get custody of my children. I couldn't stand the idea of them starving despite all I was doing by working hard to provide them with a better life.

A few weeks later, the children were on holidays, and we all agreed that they could spend two weeks at my mother's place. Two days before the agreed time, he dropped the children and one of their nannies off. Prior to that, I had sent him eight thousand dollars for the bills. He left the children at my mother's house and gave the nanny 10 dollars for their upkeep. I purposely asked to check how much he had left for the children when he dropped them off and my mother refused to tell me how much he gave them. When she finally told me after I insisted, I couldn't hold my anger. I called him and told him that the money I sent was not for him and the numerous girlfriends he was entertaining. It was first and foremost for my children. This was one of the few times I disrespected him. He went back to my mother's house and deposited an additional thirty dollars out of the eight thousand dollars he had received. I decided not to call again, rather I just told myself that there was no way a man like that would raise my children. No way!

How to get custody of my children became my number one priority after the divorce. The judge told me she would grant it to me on condition that, I could secure a job in a country where I could stay with them. My assignments so far had been in countries with limited security where I could not have the children with me. I became restless about getting a new job. God granted me favor in the sight of my boss who agreed to release me and even guided me on the official procedures to request for a station where I could have my family.

The challenge now was to find a vacant position I could go to. I knew I needed prayers for this to happen, so I took a two week leave and traveled to a place of prayer. For those two weeks, I slept in a particular church on a student's mattress. I did not go in a hotel, I prayed and slept in the church. Every night, I was asking God to open a door for me, for the sake of my children.

Two days before the end of my leave, as I was praying one night when the church's prayer group came for a vigil. They did not know me and I did not know them. Only three people from the Senior Management of the church knew what I was going through, including the lady to whom God spoke about Him permitting me to leave my marriage.

Because divorce was nothing to glory about in the church circle, they had kept my story secret. So, when the members of the prayer group approached me around 3am to ask if I wanted to share my prayer point for them to help me intercede, I politely said I couldn't share. How could I tell them that I was praying for the custody of my children in a divorce case? Their leader decided that they would pray for me despite it all.

After a few minutes, one of the ladies in the group stopped their intense prayer session and told me that she had a message from God for me. She said,

> "The Appointment I was expecting would come very soon."

What baffled me was the fact that she used the exact terminology used in my organization, which was not a terminology commonly used in my country. I knew it was God talking to me, answering me using the exact words I was using while praying to Him.

The following day, as I was going about buying the things I needed to go back to my station to resume my duties after the two weeks' leave, I got a congratulatory message from my colleague. I had just been transferred to a city where I could have my children with me.

This is how the God I call 'Jehovah Olugbeja' won the custody battle for me. The judge was overjoyed and was willing to grant me full custody of the children. A few weeks after this, I left the country and was on the plane with my children and my mother to start a brand-new life in another African city.

We settled-in quite quickly and the day my children were to start school, I stepped out to go and buy bread at the bakery for their breakfast. I heard people praying in the house opposite ours. I did not know a Pastor was living there. I did not know they had prayers from 6 to 7 am every morning. All I saw was the sticker of a renowned on the door. The Holy Spirit with His gentle still voice told me:

"Go to that church."

I will forever be grateful for the fact that I heard the instruction and the fact that I yielded to it, because this instruction saved my life and that of my children.

Let me pause here to address something about the fact that the God we serve hates divorce. I am sure some of you reading may be shocked that I said God helped me in my divorce case. Yes, He did. I prayed through every step of the process and He helped me through it. Does it mean that He supports divorce? The answer to this question is a capital NO!

My case was exceptional, it was more like a rescue mission from a dungeon where my destiny had been caged by an enemy who pretended to be a husband. That is why praying to ask God regarding who to marry is so important, because once the wrong choice is made, there is no going back. Many people are stuck in the wrong marriage without an alternative. Other people die in the marriage in the process of everything going on. Not long ago, a popular gospel singer was allegedly killed by her husband.

The story I heard about her marriage made me cry. Her ordeal was similar to mine, except that I did not allow my husband to manage all my income. The only reason I did not entrust my full earnings to him was the fact that he had already demonstrated that my children and I were not his responsibility. If he had taken care of me during the two years I was jobless under his roof, I would have probably allowed him to manage what was supposed to be our money. However, because he made it clear from the onset that his money was his money and not ours, I took the same stand with the caveat that I made sure he lacked nothing and had access to a level of luxury that he had never experienced before because I could provide, and I believed God gave it to me for the family.

I consider that God had mercy on me probably first because of the destiny He wants me to fulfill. Secondly, my life and destiny has a rippling impact on several lives. Thirdly, I believe I found mercy because of the prayers of my mother. This woman never stopped praying for me and her intercession worked. God gave me a second chance, one that majority of people will probably never have.

I am not and will never be among the people who are trivializing divorce in the body of Christ. The Body of Christ if you ask me, should never experience divorce. It is an anomaly, and the trends of increasing numbers of divorces are not a good signal. If the children of God were following Biblical instructions and living according to the Kingdom's standards, there would be no divorce in the Body of Christ . The Master is not happy with divorce, just the same way He was not happy with me dying in a marriage where I was going through hell.

My marriage by all standards was not a kingdom marriage. A Kingdom marriage is a marriage by which two people join forces to advance the purpose of their common King and Master, Jesus Christ. Kingdom Marriages do not crash, they strive, they shine, they overcome adversity in togetherness, and they are meant to last. They are founded on solid rock and the Master is their epicenter. I pray for all my children to have Kingdom marriages. Anything less than that is substandard.

Unfortunately, we have so many 'simile'- Kingdom marriages in the body of Christ nowadays. The first reason is that people who are getting married together may be Christians, but they do not understand the meaning of being citizens of the Kingdom. Christians who do not abide by the Laws of the Kingdom they profess to belong to, but rather live according to the laws of the kingdom of darkness.

Sin is a trademark of the kingdom of darkness. Lies, adultery, fornication, masturbation, etc. When a young man or a young lady is a pathological liar and never overcomes this habit before marriage, he or she might be a Christian, but not a Kingdom citizen. The fact that the spirit of lying is subduing someone is evidence that he or she is still being governed by the laws of the kingdom of darkness. When he or she gets married, that marriage will most likely not be a kingdom marriage, but rather a marriage just officiated in church as per my understanding.

The Kingdom of Light has its lifestyles, its priorities, its laws, etc. Those who do not abide by them are not citizens of that Kingdom. So, you have to first be a Kingdom citizen, then find another Kingdom citizen, and then together you will have a Kingdom marriage.

I also want to add that, people who have their marriages celebrated in church and profess to be in Kingdom marriage should not divorce, they should rather strive to become Kingdom citizens and have a Kingdom marriage even if it did not start it that way.

If you were not a Kingdom citizen and you got married to someone who was not a Kingdom citizen, you will probably find yourselves in a situation where the lifestyle of the kingdom of darkness will negatively impact your marriage. Instead of considering divorce, please first consider amending your ways together to enter a Kingdom marriage.

I was listening to a man of God recently who was explaining that the devil normally uses three categories of people. He first looks for a man with an evil heart or an evil man whose motivations are to kill, steal, and destroy just like his master, the devil. If he cannot find one, he will make use of a selfish man whose motivation is about self and self only and if none of the above is available, he will settle for a naïve individual, someone who is not motivated per se and allows him or herself to be guided by any wind of doctrine.

I believe that the church is full of naïve people who have not yet taken a clear stand to serve the Master and to align with His motivations. They are swayed by different things and follow one trend or another, they are moved by one wind of doctrine to another. They will start following ungodly friends, people without any value systems, and as a result, adopt their habits.

Unfortunately, selfish people have also found their way into churches, probably drawn by the "prosperity teachings." A quick word about what people call prosperity teachings: These teachings are not about prosperity, but about God's plans and desires for His children and how to access them. These teachings are not about becoming rich to flaunt money around; they are about God's desire to channel His wealth through people who are willing and ready to meet the needs of others.

Kingdom wealth cannot be entrusted to selfish people; the earlier people realize that, the better. Several Christians are in church because they heard God can make people rich, but instead of going through the process to meet God's requirements, they remain the same people for years. God will always look at our motivations before He answers our prayers. Many prayers are not answered because the motivations are selfish and not kingdom-motivated.

The Kingdom of God is a Kingdom where caring for others is a lifestyle. Our Master Jesus came to give His life for us. Real Kingdom people care for others, strive to see others succeed, and become the best versions of themselves.

If you are in church, calling yourself a Christian, and all you care about is you and yourself, let me burst your bubble now and tell you that you are not a Kingdom citizen, and this is probably why your marriage is suffering. Go back to the Lord and ask Him for a loving heart, and you will see how things will change. Instead of considering divorce, please check your motivations and self-assess to know whether you are a Kingdom Citizen or not.

The third category of people I call, the evil ones, are also found in the church. They are people whose motivation is to intention-ally hurt others. I believe people can easily fall from one level to another, from naiveness to selfishness to evil. That is why the Lord instructs us to guard our hearts with all diligence. A naïve heart can become selfish and later become evil.

Judas Iscariot probably started as a naïve person in my opinion. The love of money turned him into a selfish man who stole from the purse he was keeping. The devil then made an offer that was grounded on that love of money, but this turned him into an evil person because he finally betrayed an innocent man. I believe Judas did not allow evil to deeply take root in his heart because he repented from his actions when he saw the sufferings Jesus went through.

Unfortunately, several people have become evil in the church after allowing the devil to deposit more of his seeds in their hearts. I often tell people that the devil is like someone who will ask if he can deposit a few things in a room of your house because he does not have a house. The moment you say yes to him, you have granted him access to bring more stuff and the liberty to come and go to pick a few things or to add more things.

So he will start by sowing the seed of jealousy against another sister in your heart, and a few months later, you will find yourself wishing for evil to happen to the person. What seemed to be a jealous look at the lovely skirt the sister was wearing that Sunday, will progressively mature into profound hatred for her because you allowed the devil to drop the seeds of envy in your heart.

Can I say something about hating people? Hatred is a seed from the enemy. That is why Jesus is admonishing us to love our enemies. The person who is hurting you, doing you harm, is of course, an enemy, but please, even when you are praying for God to avenge you, try your best to keep your heart free from hatred because the enemy might use that hatred to sow other things in your heart. And my advice when confronted with people you find difficult to love: pray for them, God will give you the grace to love them.

I digressed from the topic I wanted to address here which is the fact that divorce can never be God's will. However, He can allow it in exceptional circumstances, when the life and destinies of his children are at stake, but I am begging you, before considering divorce, first get closer to Jesus.

A word of advice for people who already got divorced: please do not believe lies from the pit of hell that God has stopped loving you. I know what it is because I battled with guilt for months until I read a book by Kenneth Hagin named Marriage, Divorce and Remarriage.

My case was an extreme one. I believe your father progressively turned into an evil man who intentionally tried to hurt me at some point. Most of the things I narrated, made me endure because he was selfish, but then, he became something else.

Chapter Nine

HE FIGHTS MY BATTLES

I told you about the night I received the revelation about my appointment. That night, I received many other revelations from God. He used the prayer unit members of the church I mentioned earlier that I went to pray for direction.

After the lady told me what God said about my appointment, another group member told me that God showed him a man who was very angry and shouting at me, accusing me. I knew it was your father, but I did not say anything to them. He told me the man had sacrificed a goat long ago. This is how I received the confirmation that your father had indeed sacrificed the goat despite me telling him it was not even something to consider as a child of God. He overlooked my suggestions before we got married. That night, I was told that the same man had gone to consult a diviner to ask two things: either my death or that I become mad. He told me how this man would be sitting every night with a small thread in his hand, making incantations for these two things to happen to me.

When the revelation about the nomination was received the following day after I received the prophecies, I had no choice but to believe the other revelations I was told. Your father had crossed the line from selfishness to evil in my opinion. He was intentionally wishing that I died. I think he had two motivations; firstly, to make me pay for the so-called humiliation he was going through, and secondly because he knew that if I died, my organization would give him a sizable amount of money as the father of my children, who were my only dependents.

Over the years, I have met men of God or people with the gift of revelation who tell me the same things I had been told during the prayer time. If someone is visiting shrines and is asking that you become mad or die, it is probably because he couldn't achieve his first objectives, I am told he made an additional request: that I become poor.

A man of God asked me why I left all my belongings, including pictures, clothes, and underwears, when I got divorced. He told me how this husband of mine used to supply the diviners he patronized with those items and was asking them to ruin my life with their enchantments.

I told you how grateful I was for the Holy Spirit's guidance about attending my current church. I have realized that God has an ordained place of worship for each of His children, where their needs will be met. Before I understood this truth, I believed any believer could pray in any church. Still, every house of God has peculiar graces, so God will direct His children to places where graces are available to meet their particular needs.

I heard about the attacks for the first time a few weeks before we all relocated to a new country, but I did not know I needed a solid covering to shelter me from it. Now, I know that the Holy Spirit led me straight to where the spiritual covering over my life would be thick enough to shelter me from the attacks. It's been years now, and I am not mad; I am not dead, neither am I poor. Rather, the Lord has been taking me from glory to glory. I am sure your father is asking himself how all his attempts failed. My Heavenly Father has fought all my battles, the visible and the invisible ones. He has led me to the green pastures where He has been feeding me with the knowledge of Him and His ways to enable me to prevail in life. I am a witness of the goodness of God.

Besides, this church is for me and my family, here are the key things I have obtained since I became a member of this spiritual Family:

The first thing I obtained is an understanding of the power of the word of God. In the church where I grew up, the Bible was preached, and I remember a few preachings from a few pastors that impacted my life, but there was no emphasis on the power of the Word. Nobody ever told me that my prayers were to be backed by the Word of God, that God was speaking to me by His Word, that the Word of God was executed by His angels anytime I was declaring it. Nobody hammered the need for me to mediate on the Word of God to find my identity, the promises, and the principles of God. I learned all of this in my current church. I learned the importance of reading books written by anointed men of God. The book about divorce and remarriage by Kenneth Hagin, which I referred to earlier, was bought in the church's bookshop. That book provided me the light I needed to come out of the guilt of being a divorcee and start praying for my remarriage. The importance of accessing light is repeatedly emphasized in the church; without light, we cannot be called children of light. A genuine Christian is one who devours books to enhance his knowledge of spiritual truths.

My other treasure from attending this church is an understanding of Kingdom stewardship. The first Pastor who taught me in this denomination was an excellent teacher who explained stewardship with so much clarity that I enrolled in a service unit just after my first service. Since then, I have served the Lord in every capacity I was privileged to be called to. Stewardship is a great mystery in the Kingdom of God, and exposure to this truth has been a game changer. The Bible makes us understand that God is good to everyone. However, special privileges are attached to the function of servant of the Most High God. Those who serve Him intentionally, willingly, joyfully, meaning-fully, and faithfully have access to several rewards spelled out in the Bible, including blessing, distinction and exemption, honor, and promotion. For instance, Isaiah 65 has a complete list of entitlements attached to stewardship. People often quote Isaiah 54: "No weapon fashioned against me shall prosper, and I shall condemn every tongue that rises in judgment against me." People often forget to read the last verse of this chapter. It says, "This is the heritage of the servants of the Lord...." Serving God according to His will, is the best way to position yourself as a promoter of the Kingdom. When you are serving God, you are advancing His purposes on Earth. I do not understand people who have remained churchgoers for years and decades without taking the stand to serve our heavenly Father, also referred to as 'Abba.' The main reason behind this is the lack of understanding. The day someone understands all the benefits of stewardship, they cannot be an onlooker in the church.

Another reason why I will remain in this church for life because God told me that the denomination's Founder was the Prophet sent to me. Indeed, prophets are sent to specific people; if you are connected to the wrong prophet, you will probably miss it. Every prophet has particular assignments. Elijah was sent to provoke a revival in Israel and to the widow of Zarephath to command supernatural provision for her in times of famine. He was sent to Elisha as a mentor.

My Prophet was sent to me first as a covering. His dedication to God has turned him into a General in the Army of the Lord, and soldiers under his watch are safe. He has also been sent to me as a mentor for achieving a global impact. He started somewhere some decades ago, and God made him an international phenomenon with an impact on almost all the nations of the

Earth. God told me I would have a global impact when I was four years old. For this to happen, I need to follow a leader who has been there. He has also been sent to me as one of the custodians of God's prosperity agenda for the end time.

My prophet has also been sent to me as a model of a successful parent with a successful home. No amount of money or wealth will satisfy someone whose children are wayward. I am following him and his wife on that thread. I know I will have a successful home because I am following him. Finally, this man of God is sent to me as a trailblazer of successful kingdom education models. I know I have a calling in that field. It is yet to be unfolded, but he has already shown the way.

You already understand that my Prophet is and will remain my father in the Lord. I believe that people can have several mentors, but only one Father; for me, he is the one I have presently. I have several mentors whose preachings are a blessing to me, but I have only one father. I am following him as he is following the Lord. One of the primary reasons I am grateful to be where I am is that, I needed a strong covering over my head and this man of God has been playing that role perfectly.

The Lord led me to the perfect place to exercise my fingers to fight and to lift my head. One of the most significant battles the Lord won for me in this church was the one of my remarriage. I told you how, after reading Kenneth Hagin's book, I understood that God was still my Father and that He still loved me. I had some doubts about that because of the church I previously attended before. Nobody knew I was in the divorce process because I told no one. However, during communion services, the lead pastor of that assembly would scream into the microphone:

> "Do not come near the table of the Lord if you are in a divorce process! You are not clean enough to approach God's table."

He was pronouncing these words with so much disdain, and I remember how I would enter my room crying after those services, asking the Lord if He still loved me. My first communion service when I joined my current church was such a relief.

So, the light I encountered in the book shut down the voice of condemnation up, and I felt that God's will for me was to get married again. I started praying about it a few months after our arrival. We were taught in my current church that prayers are more potent when backed by God's Word. The Word of God acts like a legal statute a lawyer can use to claim things in the Court of law. God helped me to articulate my claim thanks to a teaching by one of the Pastors I listened to. It was during the Worker's meeting (another evidence of the importance of being a worker). I will never forget the title of that teaching: God will give you a quick and full reward. Using the books of Ruth and Revelations, the Man of God explained that because we were serving God, God was eager to reward us with a full reward as quickly as possible. The Word hit me so hard that I sat in the church after everyone was gone and asked God for my quick and full reward. I told Him that what I wanted was a husband because I did not want to be called a divorcee.

Right there, the Lord gave me a Word from Genesis 24. I saw here that Abraham was so anxious about finding the right spouse for Isaac. God told me:

> "If I am your Father, then believe I am more eager than Abraham to find the right person for you. Abraham was an earthly Father, so how much more do I want to give you the good things you ask?"

This Word changed everything for me, including my countenance. I stood up from that chair with complete confidence that God had settled me maritally. My Pastor back then, was leaving for a new assignment. I went to visit him and bid him farewell.

He prayed for me, using the anointing oil. He anointed me and said:

"Receive the Grace for marriage."

Because I had accepted this man wholeheartedly as a prophet, his words did not fall on the ground.

The next thing I did was to start buying stuff for my wedding. I had nobody in my mind. No fiancée. Just a brother from the choir who was harassing me to marry him, but for some reason, I did not have feelings for him, or let's say my feelings died the day I visited him, and he made sure we were left alone in his apartment to convince me to have sex with him. I fought my way out of his house untouched but vowed that I would never consider him as a potential candidate for marriage. He was manifesting behaviors that were not suitable for a kingdom citizen. I bought my marriage stuff and was expecting to meet with my life partner soon. The teaching happened in August, and so did the prayer from my Pastor. I bought the things that same month while I was on vacation. Upon my return, I pursued my engagement in the choir as usual because I understood that service was the channel God would use to bring me my quick and full reward.

During a special program in December of that year, marriage remained my prayer point number one. During the twenty-one days of prayer and fasting in January, we were instructed to pray for the Kingdom first, which I did. I had a strange dream one night. I found myself in another city in another country. I was at a crossroads when a voice told me to follow the instructions when I get there.

I did not fully understand the dream until one night, while I was praying on the subject of my marriage again, I got a call from someone who was working in that country. He was looking for a staff member to join his team. Because of the dream, I agreed to join his team. A few weeks later, I was on my way to my new assignment after all the managers involved in the decision process gave their green light. There was a possibility to have a promotion and God was granting me favor in the sight of men, including men who did not want me to evolve in my career.

I did something before I left. I made a sacrifice. It was more driven by love than by any other thing. One of the Pastors of the church had children and I saw his wife several times in the morning looking for taxi to take the children to school. In my heart, I was pleading with God to give me money to buy them a car, but I did not have the money. So, when the time came for me to leave, I thought it would be good instead of selling my car, to have it fixed and painted and present it as a gift to the Pastor. I asked the support of a trustworthy deacon of the church to whom I explained the idea. He agreed to help me identify a mechanic to fix the car and afterward give it to the Pastor.

The day before I was to leave the city, the Pastor called me in his office and asked me:

"When are you getting married?"

My response was automatic.

"December 5th."

His answer was, "It is done."

It was a strange conversation. I was in love with a colleague and my prayer was for him to marry me. When I arrived at my new destination, I explained my situation to my new Pastor, and he agreed to pray with me.

A few weeks after my arrival, the founder of the Church announced the Wonder Double Agenda which kicked off with a week of prayers. We were instructed not to pray for ourselves, but rather to focus on the Kingdom of God. My Pastor called me to tell me to follow the instruction. No more prayers about marriage, but everything for the Kingdom.

We started a massive engagement with our church going out on Saturdays for rallies to preach Jesus. After a few weeks, I had to travel back to visit my children because I was not allowed to take them to the city where I was transferred to. On Saturday, I went for the general outreach. I took a sizeable number of flyers. When the church outreach was done, I still had several of them, so I decided to come back in the afternoon to distribute all of them.

After attending to some urgent issues waiting for my attention after several weeks of absence, I went out again and spent a few hours preaching Jesus and distributing flyers. When I sat back in the car after giving the last flyer, I felt something like God's approval. Heaven was smiling on me and the feeling was so deep that I started crying in the car. This was the last Saturday of June. I travelled back to my new station during the first week of July. Two weeks later, I met with the spouse God ordained for me.

He approached me at the end of the service. A nice gentleman of a certain age. My mind never considered him as a potential husband, because he looked like someone who was married. We started talking and I asked him if he could help me to find a place to rent. I was staying in an apartment that was too expensive for me. He told me his landlady had several empty apartments where he was renting. In the course of the discussion, he said something strange. He asked me if I had traveled to the United States. I told him no and he replied:

"I will take you there."

It sounded like a promise which was funny because this was the first time we met. What I did not know was that, it was a prophecy that the Lord would fulfill in His time.

I moved into the compound where he was living, and he helped me selflessly in the process. I do not know when I started developing feelings for him and he probably does not know when he fell in love with me, but at some point, he traveled to go and visit his children. We started missing each other so much that we realized that we were in love. A few weeks later, in September, he paid my dowry, and we got married on December 5th, just as I had declared to the Pastor who received my car sacrifice.

Can I shock you? I never intentionally worked toward getting married that date. The truth is, that date was the date I had written in my notebook following the instructions of my prophet during the December Special Event. After I told the Pastor the date, I had forgotten about it, and in the process of organizing my wedding, it never crossed my mind. We planned our wedding on November 26th and for some strange reasons, my office decided to send me on a mission that week. I cried my eyes out complaining about the wickedness of men, why would they send me on a mission when I was getting married? We had no choice but to postpone the wedding and the new date selected with the Pastor was December 5th. Months later, while reading my journal, I realized that the date was set up in heaven and ordained by God the day I wrote it in the journal. The God I serve is real. I got married in December to a man I met in July and I am still happily married to this wonderful man who took me to the United States just as he said it the first day we met.

Some can think that this happened by chance, but I can tell you that this marriage is a miracle. The fact is my ex-husband cursed me and told me I would never remarry. He had one of his friends, a prophet, call me to tell me that I would go from one man to another without getting married unless I came back to his friend. I can tell you that these words were not empty. They probably backed it up with some spiritual exercise and sacrifices to empower them. So yes, there was a contention in the spirit realm against me getting married, but Jehovah My Defender, came through for me once again, against all odds, I was gloriously married in my prime even as a mother of three children.

Only the God of my Prophet could pull this out for me, so yes, I am forever grateful for the privilege to be part of a Commission of signs and wonders.

This God continued to fight for me even when I did not realize the fierceness of the battle against my life. As you already know, your father died a few years ago after he revealed what he was doing in the secret. From what I gathered from his friends, he became very sick and because they all thought he was a good Christian, they took him to a man of God for prayers. The man of God then told your father that he needed to publicly admit to things he was doing secretly if he wanted God to forgive and heal him. I received a copy of the video thanks to a common acquaintance who was in shock after listening to it. People, including his friends and family members, started reaching out to me to apologize. He admitted to so many things, including those unknown to me. In the video, he was explaining how his first sacrifice to a shrine was that very goat I mentioned earlier. He also explained how after I left him, he visited many more convents and shrines to ask for my death. When he realized he could not reach me, he started attacking my children, although they were also his children. His only aim was to affect me and he was ready to go to any extent to see me cry bitterly. He also narrated that he was warned several times by God, but his anger did not allow him to yield. You also received the video from one of your cousins, so no need to go into all the details.

I understand he rededicated his life to Jesus Christ after the confession. The Mercy of God located him in his last moments and he died a saved man. Jesus, my First Lover loved him as well. For some people, including myself, this is not fair, but I have come to realize that God's love is unconditional. He does not love me because I serve Him, He loved me even before I started serving Him, the same way He continued to love your father despite everything.

In my opinion, he died because God did not want to take a chance regarding his salvation. His surviving this sickness could have exposed him to return to his wrong deeds. God forgave him and quickly called him to His glory to save his soul.

Chapter Ten

HE IS ALWAYS THERE BLESSING ME

I feel that I have said a lot about men previously. Now, I want to focus on my First Lover, the love of my life, Jesus Christ. I did not have any idea of how deep my wounds still were. While remembering all these events, I could still feel the pains and the sadness I went through, but as I am rounding up, I want to call to mind the goodness of the God who kept me in all these trying times. The One who never abandoned me even when I distanced myself from Him. My First lover is Good indeed. He is Faithful, He is Gentle, He is Merciful, and He is Righteous. A lifetime will never be enough to know and worship Him, but then, we will have eternity for that. A this point, I would like to share a bit of what I know about Him and why I will tell people that He is worth following.

His goodness is one of the sweetest things about Him. This side of Him that will make Him have good intentions towards me and anyone else. I have now come to know that His plans for me are for good and not for evil. He will never wish me evil and will never be part of bringing evil my way. My enemies will of course try, and my own mistakes might lead me to evil, but in all this, His Goodness will always help me out. His goodness is a critical part of Him. He never dissociates Himself from His goodness anytime He is dealing with men, including evil men. He might be angry at men, but He will forever remain good to men. One may ask, how can someone remain good while angry? Have you seen parents angry at their children? Very mad because the child did something? However, except for evil ones, parents will never wish evil on their children, they will discipline and even though the punishment might look like an evil-doing from the parents, the aim will always remain for the betterment of the child. Jehovah is and will remain the best Father ever, and because He is a Father, His goodness will always come to play to the relationship He has with us.

Many might not know that, but God loves humankind more than anything else. He loved us so much that He gave His most precious treasure to redeem us. People often portray Him as a wicked entity who enjoys punishing humankind, but this distorted perception of God is because people do not know Him. Those who know Him, who have a relationship with Him know how loving He is. Because the god of this world is working hard to put a blindfold on the eyes of people, so they do not see who God is.

I really do not understand why people judge God without knowing Him. So many prejudices about someone they do not want to get close to. My point is, if you do not taste Him, you will never know that He is good.

I have personally seen His goodness when He did not allow me to die in my mother's womb or at birth despite the opposition from hell. I experienced it when He delivered me from Asthma while people thought I would have terrible crisis my entire life. I have tasted of His goodness when He opened great doors for me to study, and for me to obtain great job opportunities over and again. I have benefited from His goodness anytime I messed up and then went back to Him for forgiveness. There was not one day that He rejected me. I have lived in His goodness my entire life, and I intend to dwell in and to continue to feel it when we finally see face to face.

Another virtue of My First Lover Jesus that endears Him so much to me is His faithfulness. The Bible calls Him the Faithful. It also says that His faithfulness is great and endures through all generations. His faithfulness is the side of His character that makes Him to never give up on me. I have experienced it repeatedly. How many times did I fall short of His grace? How many times was I supposed to pay for my mistakes? How many times did I find myself on the wrong path just because I did not ask for His guidance or did not follow it even when He told me what to do? The Bible says that His mercies are new every morning and this is so true. Have you ever met someone who always sticks to you, never letting you down even when you give up on yourself? Someone who continues to believe in you even when you stop trusting in yourself? Someone who keeps cheering you up, keep telling you that you can do it even when you cannot see your own ability? Someone who will revive your dead dreams even when you have buried them under tones of excuses? What do I say about this God who has been with me through thick and thin? The one who was with me when I was crying bitter tears and was showing me His love when everyone else around me was despising me. God's goodness and faithfulness are always going hand-in-hand. I heard this from a Man of God and it blessed me so much: God's goodness is the reason why He designs good plans for us, and His faithfulness is the reasons why He helps us, sometimes in spite of ourselves, to stick to His plans. I do not even know if He was ever disappointed by me, while I disappointed myself several times. Jehovah is Faithful and my guess is, His faithfulness is just a manifestation of His steadfast love, because real love is faithful.

His faithfulness kept Joseph in the pit, all through the desert, in the house of Potiphar and in prison. His faithfulness did not allow King Saul to kill David. I believe His faithfulness is the reason why I am still alive and why my children are alive. His faithfulness took me through my academic journey. His faithfulness is the reason why He revealed Himself to Abraham, then to Isaac, to Jacob, to Joseph, to Moses, and to generations of those who considered themselves to be the seed of Abraham. One of my favorite names for Him is the Covenant keeping God. I have experienced His faithfulness times and times again. Once He makes a promise to someone, He always keeps His own part of the bargain and as long as the person stays close to Him, the promise will come to pass. 'He will never leave me; He will never forsake me.'

Another trait of Jesus my First Lover that makes me stick to Him is His mercifulness. My Jesus is so merciful. The Bible says, His mercy endures forever. It also says that, His mercies never come to an end; they are new every morning. His Mercy is this side of Him that makes Him overlook my flaws and forgive my sins and mistakes. And yes, He does that every morning! The girl talking here is full of mistakes and shortfalls. I dealt with so many issues over the years, including anger, depression, pride, etc... How He kept loving me despite all these is still a mystery to me. His Mercy made Him forgive me so many times. His mercy is the reason why I am still in His Hands after several decades of back and forth. A songwriter said, 'I could have fallen on the wayside, but I am amazed at how He showed me mercy.' This song speaks volumes about how I feel about His mercy. His Mercy will have Him look past your guilt, your shame, and even beyond yourself. Another song from someone who experienced His mercy firsthand. Considering the sinful nature of humankind, none of us could serve Him and be close to Him without His mercy. His mercy pushed Him to design clothes to cover Adam and Eve after the fall, and that's how He is still in the business of covering our shame every time and on every occasion. I am grateful for His mercies, because He covered up for me so many times. I also believe that His mercies are the reason why he allows the wicked to operate for so long. He will keep sending warning, while His goodness is hoping that the wicked will repent. But then, His Righteousness will definitely come to play at some point in the process.

Another great feature of my First lover is His Righteousness. This side of Him that makes Him perfect and fair in all His ways. This characteristic of His makes Him withstand sin and unrighteousness. He does not lie; He does not make false promises. He does not condone injustice. That's the reason why our sins are meant to bring judgment against us, but thanks to the sacrifice of Jesus and His precious Blood, that judgment was passed at Calvary. God's righteousness is the reason why He rewards both those who act right and does who do evil. The Bible calls Him the Rewarder of those who diligently seek Him. The Bible says, 'He is not unjust to forget our labor of love towards the saints.' I have known this Rewarder God for a few decades now. I saw how He kept my family just because I was serving Him with my whole heart. I can never forget how I heard His voice one morning in December a few years ago telling me: I will reveal myself as a Rewarder to you. Less than two weeks later, I got a call from someone totally unexpected, a call that changed the course of my life. I was offered a job with another organization earning almost four times what I was previously earning. He is real, which is also why someone must be careful while trying to hurt others. The Bible also speaks about the reward of the wicked. The same God rewarding good deeds rewards evil actions. The truth is His goodness, mercy, and faithfulness will give us several opportunities to repent. Still, after several warnings, if we are bent on doing evil, especially against people to stop God's intention for them, we will definitely have to face His judgment and even His vengeance. His vengeance is against those who want to stop His plans, while His judgment applies to those transgressing His laws. While His judgment is often a chastening to bring us back, His vengeance is often final with no other chance of redemption. Please never find yourself among those who are trying to stop someone who is on assignment for Jehovah, you might have to pay it dearly.

Let me end this by providing other practical advice for you to have a successful relationship and marriage when Jehovah will bring the right person your way:

First, have your checklist ready even before the person shows up: Does he love God? Does He hear God? Does he obey God when he hears Him? Is he spiritually sound enough to help you grow in your spiritual life? Does he understand that he is called to be the High Priest of your Home, and is he ready to service the altar of the Most High God? Is he God-fearing? Is he working hard-working? Is he teachable?

Does he love you? Do not follow a man who loves God but does not love you, hoping he will love you later. Someone told me recently that she assumes that if a man asks a woman to marry him, he loves her. I am sorry to contradict this, but sometimes, men ask women in marriage for other reasons than love. In my case, your biological father asked me to marry him because he saw my prospects and knew I could help him have a sweet life. Have you not heard of men marrying ladies from wealthy families to secure access to the family's assets? Never assume a man asks you to marry him because he loves you. Check it. Observe it. A man cannot hide his love for a woman. I can tell that your biological father loved Suzan because he was ready to do anything for her. In the same vein, I can tell that he never loved me because he reluctantly did anything for me. You will never have to complain for a man in love to show his love to the woman he loves. He might speak a different love language and give her gifts while she expects quality time, but he will express his love to her. Please take the time to check if he loves you; that's after checking that he loves God.

The question of his love for God is critical. Is someone showing an uncommon zeal in serving God - a lover of God? The easy way to answer this question should be YES. But unfortunately, so many people nowadays have mastered the art of eyeservice. They are swamped in church activities just like your father was when I met him. He was not a Pastor, but he was a reliable worker in the church. But nowadays, even people wearing prestigious titles such as Pastors, Prophets, and Apostles are no more lovers of God, but rather lovers of themselves. I recently heard about the story of a Man of God who killed his wife who was trying to obtain a divorce from him after he subjected her to years of domestic abuse. He did not want to allow her to have her freedom and decided to kill her. While agreeing with the fact that dedication to God via stewardship should be a pointer to one's love for God, you should also pay attention to the existence of the fruit of the Spirit in the life of the person you are considering marrying. Is he displaying God's love and its subsidiaries such as patience, kindness, gentleness, and self-control? Is he obeying God's word? It might be difficult to have all the answers to these questions in the short time you will spend trying to know your potential spouse. However, my First Lover is also searching the hearts and can tell you who a person is. Please take time to hear from Him before making any move. Needless to say, you must learn to hear Him for everything in your life.

Another criteria to check is: Does the person you want to marry have a vision? Does he know what God expects from him, and does he see a role for you in this vision? Do you see a role for yourself in fulfilling that vision? His vision might be too heavy for you to carry. In that case, are you ready to make the relevant sacrifices to build enough capacity to carry that vision?

Another question to ask is: Does he have a spiritual covering? Is he accountable to someone trustworthy? You know that our family benefits our Prophet's strong covering. This is where we belong. I can understand that God wants you to follow someone to join another family, but then you want to make sure that you have at least the same kind of covering where you are going. In fact, the first question would even be, does he even have a covering? If he does not have one, please do not follow him unless you want to be exposed, just like a house without a roof. I have also seen cases of couples meeting in a church, even getting married there, and a few months or years later, one of the spouses wants to leave the church for one reason or another. This happens to be difficult conversations. In that case, I advise the spouse not to leave unless God says explicitly so. There is a reason why God called you to be in that particular church. There is a reason why your spouse found you there and why you two were joined together in that church. Therefore, unless God specifically asks you to leave, do not leave.

Another critical question is: Do you have enough consideration for him, and can you respect and submit to him like the Bible asks you to? Something in his life must command your respect, leading you to accept his leading. This is important because submitting to a man you do not respect would be difficult. On this, it is very important that you do not marry someone with a shallow spiritual life. A spiritual woman like you cannot afford to marry someone who does not have the capacity to take her deeper in the things of God. You will be frustrated a few months into the relationship if you are not able to share with your spouse the things you are receiving from God. Please ensure you both are connecting spiritually. I have seen couples struggling to have conversations on spiritual matters because of the difference in the depths of relationships with God. As the Bible says, deep calls to deep. I can tell you that discussing with a shallow Christian when you have a deep relationship with God is kind of complicated, especially when he is your husband and is supposed to be the Head.

Other considerations that I consider subsidiary but worthy of attention are: Do you love him? Do you find him attractive? Are you ready to support him? Can you see him in the picture when you project yourself?

Here are a few pieces of advice you can consider once you are in the relationship: Never forget that Jesus should always have the first place in your heart. Never allow any man to take His place. Never allow your love for a man to take over your love for the Father. Stay connected to heaven; it will help your relationship wax even stronger.

My second advice once you are in the relationship is never to be the reason why your partner's love for God grows cold. You should pray for him, encourage him whenever he is down, and ensure he gets the peace he desires with you. You should be item number one on his thanksgiving list after his salvation.

As much as possible, your relationship should draw you both closer to the Master and not the contrary. If a relationship is drawing you far from Jesus, please check it. Besides, as previously mentioned, emotional and physical connections should not be overlooked. However, I am sharing them with you because they will help you envision the kind of home your First Lover has for you. He inspired me to pray these prayers for you and I am following His guidance:

Your home is blessed. Your home is the Kingdom of God where righteousness, peace, and joy reign. I decree that just like Ruth, you will find peace in the house of your husband.

Your Home shall be called a House of Prayer for all the nations, a place where the fire will never cease to burn on the altar of the Most High God.

Shouts of joy and victory will constantly resound in your home because of the righteousness upheld by your family.

Your home will permanently experience the grace for abundance, and you will always have all sufficiency in all things at all times.

Your home is a city set upon a hill that cannot be hidden, a place where people will glorify God because of the good deeds they will witness. Your home is forever built on the Solid Rock.

I decree upon you that you are a fruitful wine in your husband's house, just like Rebecca. You will carry nations in your womb, your mind will be fruitful, and the Lord will bless the works of your hands.

Your children will be mighty upon the Earth, the Spirit of God upon your husband's life, and your life will never depart from your children. The Word of God will never depart from their mouths. They will be a subject of constant celebration.

Your husband will love and celebrate you. He will remain the High Priest of your home, performing his duties with an unfailing consistency. Jesus will remain his Lord and Master. He will never depart from the ways of the Lord.

Remain forever blessed in the Name of our Precious Lord Jesus Christ, who will remain our First Lover forever!

www.ingramcontent.com/pod-product-compliance
Lightning Source LLC
Chambersburg PA
CBHW071442130726
47997CB00006B/2200